also by eleanor wells

All Our Yesterdays

Fairytale

ELEANOR WELLS

PUMPKIN CARRIAGE PRESS

Boulder, Colorado

FIRST EDITION

Library of Congress Control Number: 2025924149

Ebook ISBN: 979-8-9990404-6-6
Hardcover ISBN: 979-8-9990404-5-9
Paperback ISBN: 979-8-9990404-1-1

Edited by Olivia Bennett
Layout by Vellum

Printed in the United States of America by Pumpkin Carriage Press, an imprint of Cinderella Pictures LLC, Boulder, Colorado.

Cover Art by Eleanor Wells
Black and White Picture of a Man by Aliakbar Nosrati sourced from Canva

For Alex

We are such stuff as dreams are made on.

William Shakespeare

deadheads

side a

Ship of Fools

one

"Tom."

It takes Patty's voice from the backseat and her hand against my shoulder to realize the salesman is talking to me. I've just had the most exhilarating ten minutes of my life, and I want to delay the reality check for as long as possible.

"What do you think?" the salesman asks me with a hopeful but plastic grin.

"It's awesome," I say. "It drives like a dream." It's true. It does. I'd been waiting for this Oldsmobile Cutlass all my life. It was a 1974 model, one the salesman told us was practically brand new. As I run my hands down the cool, smooth wheel, I take in the sensation of leather against my back—it's the most comfortable seat I've had in months. I take a deep breath, close my eyes and imagine driving it up to Mom and Dad's as they can't help but gape and acknowledge that I've done something right with my life.

"I think your husband's in love with the car," the salesman tells Patty. She gives him a tight, tired smile.

3

"I'm not denying it," I say, still looking ahead. We don't correct him on the fact that we're not married. We don't care if people like this assume that we are—never mind that we don't have rings.

"Should we go in and talk more?" the salesman asks.

He definitely thinks he's going to close. I need to cut it now. "Can I think about it?"

We get out of the car just as a radio DJ introduces "Blue Suede Shoes." I sigh. I don't have anything against this song, but it's either been this or "Hound Dog" for the past two weeks. Elvis recorded a lot of other songs, you guys. Oh, whatever. It's a stupid thing to get mad about. I still can't believe he's gone.

Patty puts a hand on my arm and we face the salesman.

"Sorry," I tell him. "It's just, Elvis."

"I heard his girlfriend found him on the toilet," he says. "He was younger than me. Very sad."

"Makes you think about how short life is," I mutter. "I'm prioritizing things that matter."

"Like getting the right car?"

I can't help but cringe at his pivot, but I kind of led into that one.

We go back and forth about five hundred times—or the amount of time it takes for "Blue Suede Shoes" to end plus "Rock Around the Clock" and "Mr. Sandman" to play in full —about why I don't want to move forward today as the Oldsmobile's beautiful, sleek, black color and the sticker price on the windshield—$4,000—yank me in opposite directions. I could put a downpayment on it if I really wanted to, but I'd have to say goodbye to almost my entire savings for it to make sense, and even then, I'm not sure I could swing the monthly payments.

We're saved at about the time the radio cuts to a commercial break, when another young couple approaches the salesman with a question. I give Patty a look, slipping my hand into hers as a sinking feeling fills my stomach. We know we need to leave.

We walk a few steps before I realize the keys are still in my hand. I sigh and reluctantly run back to the salesman. He's busy trying to charm this couple, to make his sale, so he doesn't notice me. I have to tap on his shoulder to get his attention.

"Sorry about that," I say, handing them over.

"Hey, Tom. See you next time?"

"Sure," I say quickly, darting past the Oldsmobile and back to Patty as I take her hand again.

I look back, realizing that I hate everything about this place. I hate how they choose music like the world ended in 1959. I hate their kitschy patriotic decor—why does a dealership need that many American flag pennants? The only clue that it's *not* the 50s is the fact that cars from the last twenty years are on this lot. I might hate not having a car more, but it's not time. Not yet.

We need to get out of here.

Staying is too painful.

Anyway, who am I kidding? Mom and Dad wouldn't be impressed. More than likely, Mom would say, "Why do you need such a fancy car? Are you trying to show off?" Dad would butt in with "You're not going to sell this one for musical equipment, are you?"

Still, as we walk towards the bus stop, I tell Patty, "Someday we're going to be driving out of here in that car."

"I'm sure there's enough in savings for something, right?" she says. "We can get something basic—as long as it gets us from point A to point B."

There's exactly $1,357.43 in savings. Definitely enough for something basic, but Patty deserves better than that. "I didn't sell myself into indentured servitude to downgrade from the Datsun."

"Have you tried looking for another job?" she asks.

"Gee," I say sarcastically. "Never thought of that."

"Sorry," she says. "I could ask Diane if they're still hiring."

"I've told you, I don't want to work at the hospital," I tell her. She's only brought this up about five hundred times since Dad berated me for a minor clerical mistake in front of customers. But she's never once asked if I want to be surrounded by sickness and death on a daily basis.

We stop, pulling over to the side of the grass to let someone by. "Well, geez, don't be so high and mighty. It's something that's not your parents. Besides, don't turn your nose up at it before you ask Diane how much they'd pay you. It's probably more. And we'd get to work together. Is that so bad?"

"In completely different departments, so."

Patty rolls her eyes. "What does that have to do with anything?"

I pause, wondering if I'm being unreasonable. It's been five years since Jack died and since Cindy's injury. Still, I tell Patty, "The hospital's in Manhattan. That'd mean—"

"Yeah, *I'm* still commuting there every day."

"But you're not in the band," I say.

From the look she gives me, I know what's coming next. "Newark was supposed to be temporary."

I say nothing.

"You know, Tom, for as much as you talk the talk, I think you're a homebody at heart."

I freeze now. "What's that supposed to mean?" *I'm a homebody at heart?* Give me a break. I hate this dump excuse for a city and I always have. We moved in with Frank, Donna, and Wally because it was convenient. I can't imagine what trying to find time to practice, much less go out for gigs, would be like if we didn't live together. When Patty doesn't say anything, I add, "You want me to severely limit the time I've available to do the one thing that doesn't make me want to kill myself?"

Patty scoffs. "You're putting words in my mouth!"

As the linger of her raised voice cuts through our suburban surroundings, I realize I don't want to go down this road. I never do. "I'm sorry," I whisper.

"I just hate seeing you work so hard for... peanuts and abuse," she says, reaching her hand out to stroke my cheek. "And if there's anyone who can make things happen no matter what... it's The Hermits."

With a smile, I look into her Sinatra-blue eyes and see how the sun makes the freckles on her nose sparkle. I lied a second ago. Music isn't the only thing that makes my life worth living. It's her, too. I slide my hand into hers, kiss it, and we keep walking towards the bus stop.

When we get there, Patty inhales, and her entire face contorts almost immediately after she sits down on the bench.

I realize what's wrong when she stands up and Coke drips from the back of her white cutoffs. The stain covers her entire butt.

"At least it's not shit," I say, trying to cheer her up.

"Very funny," she remarks. With a groan, she adds, "these are the ones that Mila Potter designed for Malone's. She probably didn't design them herself. I'm sure she gave her input and posed in them, but still. They weren't cheap."

I sigh, taking off my button-up off and handing it to her. It's short sleeved so she can't tie it around her waist, but we have to work with what we have. She puts it on, which at least will cover half the stain until we get home. "It'll come out," I reassure her. Patty's always loved Mila and is always taking fashion inspiration from her.

"Yeah, I hope so," Patty mutters.

I don't have a chance to say more before I hear my brother's familiar voice, imitating our parents' snooty friends in the way we've done since we were kids. "Mr. Hargrove?"

I sigh, look up, and see my brother's orange Chevette. Rick leans over from the driver seat as Jenny waves at us from the passenger's side, the window down, balancing a grocery bag in her lap. "Mr. Hargrove," I repeat, "You know you're in the bus lane, right?"

"Where are you going? Let us take you somewhere," Rick says.

Patty silently gestures toward their car. She knows what I know, that the drive will be three times faster. But—

"Um, I just sat in Coke," Patty says.

"What?"

"She just sat in Coke," I tell Rick.

"I was wondering why you were in your undershirt," Rick tells me. I see the bus approaching about a block away. We have to hurry up. "Don't worry. I think we have a towel in here somewhere."

Rick activates the flashers as Jenny gets out.

Once I'm in, they realize they don't know where the towel

is. I hurriedly tell Patty to take off my shirt so she can sit on it, and we can wash both when we get back.

"Are you sure?"

The bus is right on our tail and honks, making us all shake.

Patty quickly follows my suggestion, and Jenny gets in after her.

The bus honks again.

"Seatbelt," Rick scolds.

I give my brother a look as we both buckle. Once he takes off, I realize Cole Porter's playing on the radio and cringe.

"Anyways. Hi Tom, hi Patty!" Jenny says.

We wave, and I turn to my brother. "You know this music hasn't been cool in like, forty years?"

He ignores me again. "We thought that was you we saw. What are you guys doing in this part of town?"

"Car shopping," I say.

"Oh. You going to get a new one finally?"

"Maybe," Patty says. "Eventually."

"Anyway," Rick continues, "where to, Bob Weir?"

"Home." I want to tell him that Phil Lesh is the bassist, but I let it go.

"You're on Darcy Street, right?"

"That's right," I say. "I'm surprised you remember."

Patty gives me a stern look and Rick does the same. "I wasn't going to say anything, but, a 'thank you for the ride and for going way out of your way to drive me home' would be nice," Rick says.

"We didn't know this was happening until about a minute ago, so," I reply.

Rick shakes his head and we keep driving.

About twenty minutes stuck in traffic later, we finally get back.

"Wait up a second," Rick tells me.

Patty kisses my cheek. "See you inside." I smile as she darts out of the car and up our stoop.

I'm still watching her as I hear Rick say, "Mom and Dad told me to remind you about their anniversary dinner on Thursday."

I turn back to my brother. "Uh... okay. What time? Where? Is Patty invited?" I already know the answer to the last. I can hear Mom saying, "We were thinking it would be just family." I guess there's a part of me that hopes their answer is going to change one day.

"I don't know. Call them."

"Sure."

STEPPING inside our shared house to the smell of incense and fresh breeze from the open window instantly makes the weight on my shoulders come off. I see the handmade art Donna got from Woodstock when she was just fifteen. As the lavender curtains filter the sun, I remind myself that this is where I was always meant to be.

Donna's sitting on the couch, wearing what Frank calls her woodland sprite dress. Her screen-printing stuff is laid out on the table. She sees us and smiles. "Hey."

"Hey, where's Frank?"

"He and Wally are at the store, but they'll be back later," she says.

I gesture to the table. "What are you working on?"

"Our poster for next weekend, but..." She stands up and

takes a step towards the kitchen.

Patty emerges then, wearing a clean pair of cutoffs and holding the dirty ones in her hand.

Donna turns to us both. "I heard about the wardrobe malfunction. Take care of that first... and if you two could... come back because I have some news. But you both have to have a joint with me first."

"I could use one," I say, waiting for her to say more.

"Me too," Patty says.

"Don't worry, it's good. Back here in... fifteen?"

WHILE I SHOWER off the day's sweat and grime, Patty scrubs her cutoffs with bleach and leaves them out in the sink. They'll be okay—we hope.

We're freshly changed and waiting in the living room while Donna's in the kitchen, getting our joints ready. "Let's get some music going!" her voice calls.

I walk over to our record collection and instantly go to *American Beauty*.

A second later, the music's started and I'm back on the couch beside Patty.

"Nice!" Donna calls.

"For old time's sake," I explain.

"It's perfect!" she calls back. "So are you guys coming on Saturday?"

"For what?"

"The Grateful Dead! They'll be in Englishtown!"

Patty and I exchange a look. It's been so long since either of us have been to a show.

"I'm not doing anything on Saturday," I tell Patty.

"Me either," she says.

"Count us in!" I call, admiring Donna's work on our blue-and-white concert poster. She'll have to fill in our abstract faces later, but I see the text: THE HERMITS: LIVE AT THE POCATELLO. FRIDAY, SEPTEMBER 2ND. 7 P.M. Beside it is a small black and white one of Denise Peck wrapped in a fur coat from her ad with London Fog that feels like it's been everywhere recently.

"Yay! Finally!" Donna returns with stuff for the joints and a piece of folded manila paper.

"Hey, they were on hiatus for like a year and a half," I say.

"And they've been back at it for just as long," Donna half teases.

"Hey, we've been busy."

"I know that, but the vibes haven't been the same without you two," she replies.

My last time must have been the Jersey City show. Ever since they started touring again, I have my parents to thank for keeping me away. Whether it was suddenly putting a bunch of work on my plate or threatening to fire me if I cut any time the Dead were in driving distance, I always saw what they were doing. Now, they have nothing to keep from a show that's an hour away on a Saturday afternoon.

"Should be fun," Donna says with a smile.

"Nice one of Denise, by the way," I say, gesturing to her screen print.

Donna shrugs. "Trying to figure out if we really look that much alike, I guess. I don't really see it."

"Calling shit," I tease. Donna gets the comparison all the time, and it's totally gone to her head.

"I don't even need her millions or brand deals. I just need to know how she plays that one solo on 'Charming Chivalry.'"

I smile as I turn the focus back to the manila paper in her hand. "Is that the news?"

I try to reach for it, but she gestures my hand back. "Not yet." She starts to roll the joints. "Now, Tom, off the top of your head, what is the most unbelievable piece of news you could imagine getting?"

"My parents have loved me all along?"

Donna sighs and hands the first one to Patty. "Cold."

"Um... we're going to move out of this house one day?"

"Getting warmer," she says, handing me mine.

"We're getting an album deal," I try.

Donna smiles. "Warmer." She sticks her joint in beneath her teeth and gives us each a light. As I take my first puff, I instantly wait for the calming effect of the grass to take hold.

"Someone responded to our demo tape?!"

Donna smiles wider now. "Ding ding ding!"

She hands me the manila paper, which Patty and I read together.

```
Attn: Donna Santos
c/o The Hermits
1249 Darcy Street, Newark, New Jersey 07105

August 26th, 1977

Dear Mrs. Santos,

I am writing in confirmation of receipt of the enclosed
demo tape, as well as your kind letter detailing your
admiration for our previous clients and outlining your
band's admirable credentials.

You must understand that we receive many such
correspondences from hopeful musicians such as
yourselves. Irrespective of talent, we simply do not
have the time or resources necessary to make everyone's
dreams come true.

However, your tape is interesting. The retailer
Malone's has partnered with us to find a talent to
produce their new jingle. The jingle will greet
customers across stores nationwide beginning this
holiday season. It's my understanding that they are
planning at least one TV commercial featuring the band.

Please call my office at your earliest convenience if
you wish to discuss further.

Sincerely,
```

Katharine York

```
Katharine York
Senior Vice President, A&R
Skylark Records
5250 Ellenwood Drive, Los Angeles, CA 90041
```

"Holy shit," I say once I've had a chance to process. "Holy fucking shit. *The* Skylark Records?"

"My celebrity twin's label? Yep," Donna says. "I talked to Kathy York and they want to see us in LA for an audition in two weeks. And guess how much the fee is if we get it?"

"A thousand," Patty says.

"More."

"Two thousand?" she tries.

"Add a zero," Donna says.

"Twenty thousand dollars?!" I repeat.

"That's just the song. Apparently we'd get, like, residuals and a licensing fee because the thing is Malone's wants the band to also write the song and they're going to pick the one they like the best. And if they do the commercial that'll be even more."

"Do Frank and Wally—" I start.

"Yeah, they know. You guys were out when we got the letter," Donna says. "I know it's just Malone's, but if we get this, this is 'quit our jobs and travel and do this full time' kind of money."

"Donna, we're going to get it. We have to."

two

LATER THAT NIGHT, we're all sitting around the table eating pizza, discussing how we're going to get to LA. Skylark isn't comping our travel, because of course they're not. If we drive, we'll be gone for two weeks minimum. There's no way Mom and Dad are going to let me have that much time off. But flights and hotels would be more outright. More money we don't have. Unless...

"We'll use my savings," I say. "That should be enough, right?"

"No, Tom, that's your car money," Donna replies. She turns to Frank and says, "There's got to be some in the Philippines fund."

Frank raises his eyebrow at her.

"That's for you two to go and meet his grandparents while you still can," I tell Donna. "Besides, look, we get this, I'll buy the Oldsmobile outright and then some."

"We can all chip in a little," Frank says.

As the conversation moves to ideas for the song itself, all of the cheese and pepperoni falls off my slice as I lift it up. Patty stares at me as I do my best to salvage it.

Things have been tense since this afternoon, and she's been practically silent since she took a phone call from her sister a few hours ago.

"I need to talk to you," she mouths.

Great. "Now?" I mouth back.

She nods.

The others watch us but say nothing as she leads me outside. It's a warm night and the sun is still setting.

"I'm sorry for the way I was acting earlier today," I say. "I know you're trying to help."

"Diane has Lou Gehrig's disease."

Her words hit me on a delay. "What?"

"She has Lou Gehrig's disease, Tom."

"What do you mean?" I repeat, still not able to believe what I'm hearing.

"I mean she has Lou Gehrig's disease."

Diane's been having muscle twitches for months, and I distinctly remember telling her not to worry about it. Even when Patty mentioned she'd collapsed at work and was going to get checked out, I thought there had to be an explanation other than... this. "She's only thirty."

"Yeah, and Gehrig wasn't that much older than her," Patty says.

"It's for sure?"

She nods rigidly. I watch the light and life drain from her eyes as she starts to cry. I wrap my arms around her. "They gave her two years."

"Well, hey, people live a lot longer than that these days," I say, although I can't help my own fast-beating heart. "That's what Stephen Hawking has, right? He's still going strong."

"He's an exception," Patty mutters.

I hold her tighter. "Did she say anything about what she wants to do?"

"Well, we didn't talk about it much," Patty says. "There's not much she really can do. She did say she was going to still come to your show on Friday so I guess she'll tell you more then."

I keep my eyes on Patty as I wait for her to say more.

"So, yeah, I'm going to have to stay," she says. "Gracie's going to be around, obviously, but this way I can look after the house, too. And you guys are going to be great. I know it."

I manage a reassuring look as I take Patty's hand, and we walk back inside.

IN MY DREAM, I stand outside of a massive venue. It's the Civic Center in Providence, Rhode Island.

It's a perfect, sunny day and I've just gotten there. I have my ticket in hand and plenty of time to get to my seat.

There's a crowd gathered, waiting to go in. But it can't be for the Dead. There are young girls everywhere. I'd be surprised if anyone here is past high-school age.

This is where I was supposed to go. I know it. I look at my ticket again to confirm the details.

"Well, if it isn't the man of the hour!" a girl exclaims. I turn. She's standing by herself, away from the crowd. She and I lock eyes for a moment, and her smile fades. "I'm sorry, I thought you were someone else."

. . .

As I awake with a cold sweat, something about the dream lingers, although I'm not sure what. I turn over to see it's just before three in the morning.

Patty stirs. "Tom," she whispers.

I bring her into my arms. "I didn't wake you up, did I?"

"No." She fully opens her eyes and looks at me. "I haven't slept at all."

I sigh. "Are you sure you're going to be alright here on your own?"

"I'll be fine," Patty says.

I run my fingers through her light-brown hair. It's at moments like this I can't believe how lucky I am that she's mine, and how I could get used to her always being by my side. "We don't have to go to LA," I say. "There'll be other opportunities. Besides, I think Malone's is hardly anyone's idea of the band's dream."

Patty gives me a look.

"What?"

"You're going to regret it if you don't."

"How do you know?" I ask.

"No matter what happens, in five years, even ten or twenty, do you want to be asking what if?" she asks.

I have nothing to say. Patty knows me too well. "As long as you're going to be okay," I whisper after a beat.

"Don't worry about me," she replies.

She lays her head on my shoulder. As I wrap my arm around her and bring her close, I take a moment to feel the warmth of her body against mine. It's quiet, it's still, it's peaceful. The slight breeze that comes in through our open window brings a piece of this beautiful night right to us. We drift back to sleep to the sound of crickets.

three

ON THURSDAY, I'm sitting across from my parents, brother, and Jenny in a booth at the back of Grimm's Steakhouse. They've been droning on about different types of mulch for the past fifteen minutes, and it doesn't seem like the conversation is going to end any time soon.

The stone walls and cast-iron fireplaces are supposed to make it feel like you're in the woods somewhere, and while it is nice—the relaxing trickle of the wall fountain at least makes this dinner somewhat bearable—I still would rather be in the woods than at this table.

As the four of them talk, I think about what Jack would say about the restaurant if he were here. Something to the effect of "I don't think anyone actually has a good time there. It's in the name, right?"

I'm brought back by my mother's voice. "Thomas."

I look up.

"Jenny asked you a question."

I turn to my sister-in-law. "I'm sorry, I didn't hear what you said."

"How's Patty doing? I feel bad that we didn't get to talk much the other day."

"The other day?" Mom cuts in before I answer.

"We ran into them at the bus stop," Rick explains.

"She's alright," I say. "Thanks for asking. And for the ride."

"Was Patty able to get the stain out of her cutoffs?" she asks.

"Almost," I tell Jenny. "Hoping it'll take one more wash to get the rest."

"What happened?" Mom asks. Even though he doesn't speak, I feel Dad's disapproving eyes on me too.

"Someone spilled Coke at the bus stop and Patty sat in it," I reluctantly tell my parents. I know Jenny means well, but this is just going to give them one more thing to use against me.

"Hmph," Mom replies. "Maybe, if you had a car, you two wouldn't be in this situation."

"They're cutoffs," I say, getting more irritated by the second.

"Are you going to offer to replace them?"

"I don't know!" I snap.

Good lord, there are bigger fish to fry in this world than a fucking pair of stained cutoffs.

"Thomas," Mom says. "You have been very rude and disrespectful this entire night."

Then don't talk to me like I'm a fucking child. "Sorry, mother," I manage in my best obedient-son voice.

Mom rolls her eyes.

"Anyways," I continue, "we were at the dealership the other day when they picked us up. We're working on it."

"Might I remind you that you *had* a car—which your father and I spent a lot of money on—but you decided to sell it for musical equipment," Mom says.

"It's called a bass guitar, you know," I say.

"For your escapades with Jack?" Dad interjects. "How did that turn out for you again?"

As I plunge my knife into my steak, Mom gasps and everyone stares as juice comes flying, although, thankfully, none escapes my plate.

"Anyways, Jenny," I say. "I'm glad you care more about my life than anyone else at this table."

"Thomas, that's unfair," Dad says.

"Is it?" I challenge. No one says anything, so I continue. "Diane has Lou Gehrig's disease. So, there's been a lot of uncertainty."

"Diane? Patty's sister?" Mom asks.

"Yes, Patty's sister," I snap.

"The lesbian, right?"

"What does that have to do with anything?" I ask once I've had a chance to process.

"I'm just trying to place her, Thomas," Mom says.

"That is correct," I say. "She also became Patty's sole guardian when she was twenty years old and their parents died in that car crash. Remember? We've only talked about this like five hundred times."

Mom and Dad stare at me.

"Diane is her only family," I say slowly, like my parents are five years old.

The silence continues.

"Did you not hear what I just said? She has Lou Gehrig's

Disease! She's going to die! So, I am sorry that I am a little bit mentally preoccupied."

"Thomas," Mom says. "There's no need to get upset."

With that, I stand up. "I'm going to the bathroom."

I walk towards the exit for some fresh air. I need even half a minute alone from these people.

The front exit of the steakhouse immediately breaks the immersion, as I'm met with the busy city street and zooming cars.

Yet, the evening summer air is nice. I take a moment and breathe it in.

I can't wait to be on the other side of the country.

Growing up, I used to think there was something wrong with me. It took that first Dead concert to realize there never was. I hate being reminded of how I used to feel. I lean against the wall and take a few more breaths before I hear my brother's voice.

"This isn't the bathroom," he says.

I sigh and scoot over to make space for him.

"I'm sorry about Diane," Rick mutters.

"Yeah, it's fresh, so I still haven't fully processed it myself," I say.

"Everyone's cooled off if you want to come back in," he says after a beat.

"Are you sure?"

"You know, Mom and Dad are really happy you showed up, okay?" Rick says.

"They have a funny way of showing it."

Rick says nothing.

"Anyways. I have good news to share, too. Not that Mom and Dad will see it that way, but, you know..."

Rick's face tightens. "Why don't you come on in and share it?"

LATER THAT NIGHT, the five of us—Donna, Frank, Wally, Patty, and I—are together again. We've just settled our plans to get out to LA. I ended up using a part of my savings to get us flights and a week's stay at a hotel. They didn't want me to at first but I insisted. Besides, if we get Malone's, that's $20,000. Even split four ways, it'll make $1,300 feel like a drop in the bucket.

I've got a little over $700 left now. We haven't booked our returns yet on the off chance we happen to pick up any gigs while we're there.

We celebrate by taking acid and blasting the band that brought us all together in the first place. "All Dad had to say is 'how much does it pay?'" I tell them as the tab dissolves onto my tongue. "Why is that the first thing he always goes to?"

"Because he's a fucking straight," Wally says.

"And when we get this gig, and you make a shit ton of money, isn't it going to be so satisfying to have proven him wrong?" Frank exclaims.

"It sure is!" I yell. Patty smiles at me, so I bring her into my arms, kissing her deeply.

"We're playing the wrong music, guys," Donna says. She takes the Dead off the record player. I know what she's going to put on before she does: The Mamas & the Papas. "California Dreamin'."

Perfect.

I close my eyes, lean back into my chair, and let the acid take hold of me.

Nothing else matters.

ON FRIDAY, I go through the motions, just like I always do in the rest of my life, the one where I'm not playing music and not with the people I love most. It's a particularly slow day and I'm zoned out, allowing myself to picture it. Me and Patty on a beach somewhere, enjoying life, not just surviving.

Things are better by the time we finally get to the gig.

The restaurant has an old-timey pub atmosphere and is actually pretty full. Still, only a handful of the audience actually listens. When The Hermits first formed, those kinds of performance settings were invigorating. Everyone had started out like this before they eventually went on to bigger and better.

Now, it irritates me, especially with such a big opportunity just out of reach. I wonder about what will happen if we don't get the Malone's gig. That is a possibility. The details Donna got from Kathy were vague, but it sounded like we were far from the only band auditioning. They go with someone else, and it's just back to this and it's God knows how long until the next opportunity comes around. *What if it never does?*

I finally notice Diane sitting at one of the back tables after we've finished, as Donna, Frank, and Wally have started to load the bus.

She looks beautiful and put together in the silver-blue dress she wears over a white, long-sleeve shirt and knee-length boots. Her light-brown hair is long and shiny as ever. We catch eyes. She takes a sip of her beer and waves. I notice her painted, red nails as she gestures me over. I hug her tightly.

"Hey, handsome," she says. "What are you drinking?"

"Please, let me get this," I say, sitting down.

Diane scoffs. "Nope. It's bad enough with my sister but it's even worse with you."

"What are you talking about?"

"Your pity. I don't need it, okay?" she says sternly.

I purse my lips. "PBR, then. Thank you."

As Diane goes to the bar to order it, I watch the new act walk on stage. Between the girl's long white-blonde hair, silver dress, and white makeup, she looks to be not of this earth. She begins an acoustic cover of "Starman." Her voice is soft and airy. It reminds me of Joni Mitchell's. It's good, even great. It makes me wonder if The Hermits stand out in any sort of way, or if we're just another band.

Diane comes back to the table a moment later. She watches too. "So, I hear you're going to LA for an audition?"

"It's to do the new Malone's jingle," I say with a laugh.

"No kidding," Diane says.

"We'll see," I say. "Anyway, you look good. You seem good."

"I feel good," she replies.

"Got it. Good to know," I say, taking a long drink of my beer. "Is there anything we can do?"

Diane gives me a tired smile. "Yes, actually. You can ask my sister to marry you."

I blush. "What?" A month ago, things were so stagnant. I remembered wishing that anything would break up the monotony. Now too much is happening all at once.

"Don't give me that look," she says with a teasing smile. "Don't tell me you've never thought about it. Or you and she have never talked about it."

"Well," I say, feeling my cheeks go hot, "I don't think I'm really in the position to do that for her, right now."

"You know you're the world to her, right?"

"You and her were doing just fine before I showed up," I manage.

Diane gives me a tight look. "We were surviving. I really want her to *live*, Tom. I want you both to live."

"We are," I say. "We're trying to. But I want to establish myself first, I guess."

"It's not about that," Diane says coolly.

I find myself blushing again, as the silence that follows at the table lingers. Diane's looking at me as if I'm the one that needs assurance, not her, and it's too much for me. I resolve this by looking down into my beer glass. "You know, there's been a lot of development..."

Diane shakes her head.

I look up at her, into her eyes. Suddenly, I think about the first time that I ever did, at that Dead concert in the summer of 1974.

"Well," Diane had said. "It's not going to sprout legs, is it?" She had been referring to the beer Patty had just offered me after noticing I was staring at their cooler.

She'd been so effortlessly cool that I knew I was going to have to be my very best to be worthy of dating her sister.

The thought of her body slowly failing her is something I can't fathom.

"What about Gracie? Is she helping?" I ask.

Diane nods. "Yeah. She's great. She wanted to come today, but she ended up booking a client last minute. Extended family photos, so it's good work. But she does want to come to the Dead tomorrow, if you'll have her."

"I think we'd love that," I say.

We're quiet for a moment, and then she says, "I have had a beautiful life. I have very few regrets. I just want to make sure the people I love most in this world are happy."

I nod.

"By the way, Patty said you two were talking. We are still hiring for a new accountant, if you're interested. It'd be a junior position but you just say the word."

"Oh yeah?"

"Do you want to know how much it pays?" Diane asks, slightly teasing.

"Sure."

"I talked to my boss and based on your experience and degree, he'd be able to start you at 9k a year," she says.

I blink. That's twice what I get paid at the store.

"Besides, there's plenty of opportunities to grow if you do a good job, and I know you will."

I think about what I would do with double the income. A part of me thinks I shouldn't accept too soon. If all goes well, I won't even need a day job. "That's very generous. Let me think about it."

"Of course," she says. "By the way, have fun tomorrow. I'm sad I'm not going to be able to make it."

"Here's the plan," I say. "We're going to write a letter to the Dead. Tell them what's going on. We'll get all of Gracie's pictures and films of concerts past to Garcia. He'll love it. Next thing you know, you two will be guests of honor on tour and you'll never miss another show."

Diane laughs. "Do you have a direct line to Jerry Garcia, Tom?"

"There's many things you don't know about me, Diane Reilly," I tease.

"Like she's the only one that takes pictures," Diane says with a smile. "No, I think my Deadhead days are done. But those were good memories."

"Yeah, they were."

four

FINALLY, it's Saturday, and we're all sitting on the stoop, waiting for Gracie. It's a sunny but crisp afternoon. I'm eying a single red leaf, thinking about the season to come, as her Lincoln Continental pulls up.

We watch in awe as she parallel parks it into a single spot that's happened to miraculously be available right in front of our house. As she smiles and waves at us, I find I'm laser focused on the car. She's had it for as long as I've known her. While I've always thought it was nice, in this moment it seems especially magnificent. Its shiny black body without a scratch, silver trim—it's as classy of a car as she is a person. Gracie's always been humble about the fact that she does well for herself, and while I'm not jealous, I'm ready for it to be my turn.

Gracie gets out, getting two bags of camera equipment from the front seat.

"You brought the full haul," I tell her.

"It's just my camera and a tripod," she says with a laugh. "I thought I could film a little sendoff for you guys. This is so huge!" She gives me a hug first. "Good to see you, Tom."

As Patty stands up, the two squeeze tightly. It's not long before both are crying.

"We're going to get through this, okay?" I hear Gracie whisper.

Patty gives her a nod.

After we let their moment pass, Frank gets her attention. "We could take your car to Englishtown," he teases.

"Haha, very funny," Gracie says. "After that parking job I just pulled off?"

"Hey, try doing it with the bus," Donna cuts in.

"She parallel parked our bus *one time* like two years ago," Wally tells Gracie.

"Think it's gotten to her head just a bit," I add.

"Just a little, tiny bit," Frank interjects.

Donna turns to us. "Hey. Have any of you ever done it?"

We're all quiet.

"Didn't think so." She bites her lip and steps closer to Frank, interlacing her fingers in his.

Gracie's laughing. "Glad you guys are in good spirits. Where is the bus, by the way?"

"Three blocks down, not too bad," Donna says. "There's supposed to be a hundred thousand people at this thing. It's a miracle we all got tickets."

"For sure," Gracie says. "I think I'm going to be sitting separately from you guys but we'll find a meeting spot."

"Us too, actually," I say. Patty and I had to go with the first available seats, and I don't think they're anywhere close to where Frank, Donna, and Wally are going to be.

"I guess this is the place to be," Donna says.

As her and Gracie chitchat, I eye her Lincoln again. Our teasing has made me realize something I can't believe didn't register before.

If—no, *when*—I get the Oldsmobile, there is no way I am dealing with the nightmare that is street parking on our block. Which means we'd have to move out. Which I don't want to do, or think about doing. Not until I'm better off.

Fuck.

"Ground control to Major Tom," Donna's voice calls, snapping me out of it.

Everyone's gathered on the block and ready to start walking.

Patty looks at me with a tired smile and extends her hand. I squeeze it and we all start to walk.

THERE MUST BE tens of thousands of people already there by the time we arrive. We eyed the massive crowd as we came in and were lucky to find parking on the street about a mile away. As soon as we get out, two guys, both college aged from the looks of it and dressed in Dead T-shirts, pass by.

"Sweet ride," one of them, long-haired and mustachioed, says. He's gesturing to our VW bus, decorated with shooting stars and surrounded by a whirlwind of red, white, and blue lightning bolts and skulls.

"Thanks," Donna says. "I painted it myself."

"We drove up from Tampa," the other guy with short, scruffy hair says.

"That's intense," Gracie replies.

"Eh, it was sixteen hours, and we took shifts," the long-haired one says. "Besides, worth it."

"Yeah, it is," I say, feeling my excitement spread.

"I can't speak for them, but longest I've done is Cleveland," Gracie tells them.

"She and I did Iowa City a few years back," Frank says, putting his arm around Donna and stroking her shoulder. "Knew she was the one when we could survive a road trip that long together."

We end up walking towards the venue together—Raceway Park, the first racetrack concert I've ever been to—and parting ways once we get there to stake out our spots to wait. The guys told us their names, but I've already forgotten them. We'll never see them again, but that doesn't change the fact that we connected. So easily too, and without any expectations.

That's what I love about the Dead.

We take a minute, standing in the sea of people. The familiar scent of grass overtakes my nose as we try to eye a spot for us to land. But that's going to be challenging here.

I hear Donna shout something to Frank, but she has to repeat it because of the noise. "Do you ever think we'll have crowds this big?" she repeats.

"Maybe!" he exclaims, taking her in his arms and kissing her.

"Ow, ow," a random passerby remarks.

Someone else in the crowd calls in our direction. "Rice? Is that you?"

"Hey, Gary," Wally says, biting his lip.

Gary steps forward. He's a preppy type, from the way he's dressed—crew cut hair, button-up, slacks, and carrying two beers. "What are you up to?"

"Seeing the show," Wally says. "These are my friends." We all wave as he introduces us.

"Just your friends?" Donna says with a raised eyebrow.

"We're in a band."

"No shit, what do you play?" Gary asks. He takes a step forward and joins our circle.

"Drums, like always," Wally says.

"Hell yeah, Little Drummer Boy," Gary replies.

"Those both for you?" Wally says, gesturing to the beers.

"Oh, nah, the other one's for Sue," Gary says. "Yeah, we've got a kid now and everything. Laura. She's three. It's crazy. Anyways, this is my first Dead show. I'm so excited. Sue got me into them like, two months ago."

"Wow," Wally says.

"Anyway, good to see you," Gary says. He waves and walks off into the crowd.

"I fucking hate that guy," a pale-faced Wally tells us once he's out of earshot. "Made life a living hell because I was in the marching band. There's a reason I didn't want to bring up the band, Donna."

"Oh," she whispers. "I'm sorry."

He waves her off.

"Hey," Gracie cuts in. "Let's find a place, shall we?"

WE END up having to migrate down the street so we can actually hear ourselves think, but the chatter and chaos is still very much present in the background.

Gracie sets up her tripod. "Alright, Hermits," she says. "Just speak up and we'll be fine."

I put my arm around Patty as we file in front of the camera.

"This is Grace Andreessen, live for an exclusive with The

Hermits," she narrates in a Barbara Walters impression. "Where are we?"

"We're in Englishtown, New Jersey, waiting to see the Grateful Dead," Donna exclaims.

"Would you and your bandmates like to introduce yourselves, Mrs. Santos?"

We go through it. Frank, guitar, lead vocals. Her, keyboard. Me, bass. Both of us, backing vocals. Wally, drums. We all look and realize Patty's been in frame the entire time.

"She's an honorary Hermit," I say.

Patty blushes and she and I exchange a smile.

"I hear you have an audition for Skylark Records," Gracie continues.

"We sure do!" Donna exclaims. "Watch out, world!"

As Gracie cuts the camera, a woman who's clearly already on a trip gets our attention. "You're in a band?"

"We sure are," Frank says.

"Do you have any albums out?"

"Not yet," Donna tells her. "Someday, though!"

"Oh my gosh," the woman exclaims. "Let me know!"

As her friends usher her forward, I can't help but smile. It's good to be back.

"What? Isn't it good?" Jack asked me on a warm fall night in 1970.

We'd just finished listening to *Anthem of the Sun*. "It needs to sink in."

"You can at least say *something*."

"Jesus, Jack!" I snap. "Give me a chance to think."

I'd been in a bad mood that day. Cindy had left that

morning for a meeting in DC. She and I had a nasty spat in the Newark High parking lot when I'd complained about how often she was gone and how little time she had for me. Then I went to class, only to find out I'd flunked my first test in Intro to Accounting. I was still living at home then, and I'd tried not to bring it up to Mom and Dad, but they'd probed anyway at dinner and a fight had predictably ensued.

Jack had been pestering me for weeks about listening to this band called the Grateful Dead. He wasn't working that night, and I knew damn well he didn't have anything else going on. So I took the opportunity and drove my Datsun over to his apartment.

"This is like, put together from live shows and recordings, but man, we've got to see them live. That's what everyone says, that the albums are just a commercial for the concerts," Jack told me, cutting through the silence.

"Yeah, you've said that like five hundred times already," I snapped.

Jack gave me a look.

"I've been busy with class," I said, "and trying to get my parents to piss off."

"Hey, get a job and you can move into your own apartment. Heck, we'll get one together. Not this one, obviously. We'd need another bedroom."

"I'm not moving in with you," I said, my tone still harsh. "How about you go to college so you can defer?"

"The draft? What the fuck? We're just listening to music."

PATTY'S HAND on my shoulder brings me back into the here and now. I'd zoned out in my grass-induced haze. We're in the very back row, and the band themselves are the size of pinpricks, but it doesn't matter.

I don't know if The Hermits will ever play stages this big, full of so many people from every imaginable walk of life all brought together by our music. I don't know what's going to happen in LA. But for now, it's really nice to be a part of something.

five

Six days later, we're on the plane and my last conversation with Diane has been ringing through my head. I could be making 9k a year.

If you did a good job, and I know you will, had been what she'd said.

Maybe I'm not a piece-of-shit loser after all. It seems like things are going to finally start going right—one way or another.

I sit by the window, looking out at the cloudy sky. Wally's beside me, reading Michael Rooney's autobiography for the second time while Frank and Donna are elsewhere on the plane. I feel guilty for leaving Patty and being so far from her and Diane. While they both told me not to worry, I can't help myself from doing so.

The trip doesn't feel real, and I'm not really sure what to expect.

"Pick up anything new this time around?" I ask Wally.

He takes a minute and closes the book, holding his place

with his thumb. "Oh, yeah, he's a very good writer. I can let you borrow this when I'm done, if you want."

"Sure."

"Yeah, he's just..." Wally dog-ears the book and puts it in his seat pocket. "Talking about the time he first met Sheila."

I snort. "Okay."

"It was at the Chateau Marmont. Isn't that funny?"

I shrug.

"We should go there," Wally says. "Sit at the bar, get some nice drinks, pretend like we fit in there and see who believes us. Like Donna says, act as if?"

I hardly know anything about the Chateau Marmont, only that it's a place where a lot of rich and famous people hang out. "Sure. We can ask them when we get off."

SOMETHING IS NOT JUST different but better from the second we step off the plane and are greeted by the signs that welcome us to Los Angeles. From the sun to the smiles, the bright colors, and the fact that people actually stand up straight, maybe everyone really is happier here.

It's only about ten in the morning, local time. We have the entire day to soak in the city.

Donna thinks the Chateau Marmont is a great idea. As we all stand around in a semicircle and discuss it, a young couple stops to stare. Their focus is on Donna, with her white fringe vest, matching blouse, denim cutoffs, and round sunglasses resting on top of her head.

"Sorry," the boyfriend says. "We thought you were Denise Peck. You look just like her."

"Thank you so much," Donna says.

"You really do," the girlfriend adds.

"The only difference between me and her is millions of dollars," she says with a wave of her hair.

This makes them both laugh as she slides her sunglasses down to her face.

"Anyway, have a great day," the boyfriend says with a slight wave. He and his girlfriend go along their way.

"It's a sign," Donna announces, straightening her posture and taking Frank's hand. "Skylark, here we come!"

FIRST, we head to the hotel that we're actually staying at. We booked it in Eagle Rock, because it was close to Skylark and affordable. The whole cab ride there, I can't help but notice how much brighter and sunnier everything is. Knowing that "California Dreamin'" was written when John and Michelle Phillips were living in New York makes the song make so much sense. Everything here is much more open and free. The hills, the flowers of every color, and, of course, the palm trees are all amazing.

Still, close to the hotel, I can't help but notice when we pass Cindy's Restaurant, its sign prominent above the green and white building. Even here, I can't escape my past.

Once we check in, it doesn't take long for a problem to emerge. We're right off of a major road, and that's going to make practicing extremely difficult if not impossible. Our audition is set for two days from now, and we need to have a solid version of the song by then. It was hard to find time beforehand when Mom and Dad—I swear to God, purposefully— suddenly had a ton of work to keep me at the store past seven every night. We're heading up to our rooms when a screaming boy darting down the hall nearly runs right into me. I say little as his apologetic father gets him under control.

"Cute," Frank says dryly.

We continue on to our rooms. They're fine, even though the paint on the walls is peeling and mustier than the stock room at the hardware store, but I wasn't expecting luxury. What really makes me want to pull my hair out is that I barely have a second to hear myself think before a loud group pounds their way through the hall like they're the extended family of the giant from Jack and the Beanstalk.

A week in these conditions.

I'm panicked again. What have we gotten ourselves into?

For the time being, however, we cast that all aside and pretend we're living the life we've always dreamed of. We're all dressed and ready to go before we realize we're going to need to pay for the afternoon out at the Chateau.

I finally tell them I'll use my savings for it. I brought all with me on the trip in case of any emergencies. This might hardly qualify as one, but it'll be nice to just relax for once.

Dressed in our best, we pile into a cab there.

I've never been anywhere like this place in my entire life. The tall arched windows, tiling and old-fashioned light fixtures remind me of pictures I've seen of the interiors of royal palaces. The kinds of mansions movie stars used to live in, too, if there is much of a difference. We've barely had a second to admire it when I realize that there's another problem.

You need to be a guest to get in to the bar.

We probably should have thought about that before we went to all this trouble.

Before anyone can try their hand at an excuse, I step

forward to face the impatient concierge. Suddenly, the four of us are checking in to a suite for the night and I'm out $300.

"You really didn't have to do that, Tom," Frank says.

"Hey," I tell the others. "I wanted to do it."

Wally, Donna, and Frank go back to the hotel to get our stuff while I stay.

As I WALK into the room, more neutral in color but still just as nice as the main areas, I'm immediately hit with buyer's remorse.

We're actually going to have some peace and quiet to get this song done.

But tomorrow, it'll all be gone and I'll still be out $300.

I flop onto the greenish-brown couch and close my eyes. As I listen to the faint sounds of birds and the summer breeze, I try to think about Malone's and what it means to me. Not that I ever would have had such an attachment to a national department store chain. I've been there so many times without a second thought. There has to be something we can write about.

It comes to me about a moment later. I was fifteen and Rick was twelve, and I had taken him there to get a new bike. I don't remember many specifics. It was an uneventful day. Summer. I remember because when we got home that evening, we'd eaten dinner outside. Dad grilled burgers and hot dogs. Jack had come over, too, and he'd brought Cindy. Of course I'd always known her, but as my best friend's kid sister, not a girl who'd be at high school with us come fall. There was a way the low sun had made her teased hair look like gold. I'd felt like I was seeing her for the first time that day.

They'd both come with us to see *You Only Live Twice.* Everything had gone exactly how it was supposed to. No fights. No disagreements. Things wouldn't really get bad until that fall.

Malone's. Family. The connection's there, but I need Frank and Donna to help me bring it together.

Eventually, I stand up and wander towards the pool.

Living in the moment is so underrated. There's nothing quite like forgetting about your troubles, breathing fresh air and knowing that you're alive. I feel it as I sit at the Chateau's poolside bar with a Sparkle. I knew it was a reference to Karen Richardson. I read about her once in a book about infamous Hollywood crimes. She wanted to be an actress and ended up a call girl. She'd called herself Sparkle because she always wore glittery eyeshadow and costume gowns to match. I saw a picture in that same book—no makeup, normal clothes—and she looked like any other girl.

In between sips, I look down into the blue concoction, with its lemon peel and rose petal garnish and wonder what it must be like to be murdered at nineteen only to have your legacy carried on in a drink.

Sitting kitty-corner from me is a man in a suit, drinking what appears to be an Old Fashioned. Who drinks an Old Fashioned outside on a hot day like this? He's clean cut, his hair salt and pepper and slicked back. His watch looks real gold. Even his wedding band is thick and pronounced, like it was meant to draw attention to itself. Everything about this man seems stuck in the 50s. He's like a stereotype of what I imagined successful men to be when I was a kid.

He's writing on a yellow legal pad. I can't tell exactly, but it seems to be some kind of math calculations. After a moment, he must notice me watching him and looks up.

"Hi there," he says, giving me a wry smile.

"Hey," I reply, straightening the sleeves of my purple button-up and patting some fuzz off of my corduroys.

The man gestures to his legal pad. "The work never stops."

As my hands clasp my drink, I give him an exaggerated nod. "I know how that is."

"What is it you do?"

I rush another swig of the Sparkle. "I'm a musician."

The man's eyes widen. "Oh, really?"

I force myself to look away from him as I answer. "Yeah, I'm in a band."

He sets his pen aside and leans to me now. I catch my breath, knowing what he's going to ask before he does. "Have you recorded anything that I might have heard?"

"No," I say, taking another drink. "Not yet, anyway."

"Don't worry about it," the man says. "You're young."

"Yeah, we're actually just getting started, so," I lie.

"And we all have to start somewhere," the man says with a smile. He extends his hand. "Rupert Morris."

His name is so familiar to me, but I can't place it. "Tom Hargrove," I say.

"I'm in A&R at Skylark Records," he says.

Shitfuckshit. All I can manage is an "um" before I trail off. I feel like I'm about to have a heart attack. There's a million ways I could handle this, and none of them seem right.

I don't have the chance. Rupert's distracted. It's the reason why that makes me remember why his name was so familiar.

I see her walking right in our direction. She's dressed in a white halter top, sheer lace kimono, and faded blue cutoffs. Her curled, red hair is loose, and her eyes are hidden behind orange circular sunglasses. The diamond ring on her finger rivals his in gaudiness.

Denise Peck doesn't acknowledge me as she approaches and kisses her husband and takes a seat next to him.

"What do you want, baby?" he whispers.

She looks over at me. "What is that?"

I realize Denise Peck is talking to me, and I jump. Her sunglasses are on top of her head now as she looks over at me. Of course, I see Donna in her, but I really notice her freckles and her rich brown eyes. Everyone always told stories about both, and man, I really see why. "Brown Eyed Girl" must have been written about her. Of course, "Denise," that one Randy and the Rainbows song, too.

Why is the genius singer-songwriter behind *Blue Roses* and *Castle Hymns* talking to me?

"Hello?" Denise says.

"Sorry, it's a Sparkle," I say, immediately taking another long swig. I'm almost done with this, but I'm definitely getting another.

Denise turns to Rupert. "I'll have that."

"Sure." By the time he's flagged the bartender down, Rupert watches me finish mine. "Hey, Hargrove?"

I look back at him, and then to the hotel entrance. The others have to come back sometime soon. "Yes?"

"Let us get your next one," he says.

"Uh..." I say. A part of me wants to protest, to pretend like it's no big deal, but after how much I spent on the room, I'm not going to say no to a free drink. "Thank you."

"Tom's in a band," Rupert says to Denise.

Denise lights up. "No way. I knew cool people hung out here. What's your band called?"

"The Hermits," I say.

"Love it," she replies. "I'm Denise, by the way."

"Yeah," I say, blushing. "I know."

There's something about the way her face falls and her tone drops that isn't lost on me. "Of course you do," she whispers.

"Yeah, actually, our keyboardist, she gets mistaken a lot for you."

"Really?" Denise says. "And she plays keys too? I want to meet her."

I look back towards the hotel doors. "The rest of them are out and about. They'll be back soon."

She laughs. "What do you do? In the band, I mean."

"Oh... bass." I feel myself blushing again. *Please guys, come back soon.*

"I want to know all about The Hermits," Denise says. "When did you start? What kind of music do you play?"

I catch my breath as the bartender brings two Sparkles, one for me, one for Denise. Rupert finishes his Old Fashioned, stands up, and places his hand on Denise's back.

"I'll see you later, okay?" he says, kissing her cheek.

"Sure."

He turns to me. "Nice to meet you, Tom." He walks off. I wonder if he'll have any part in our audition. Either way, we'll find out soon enough.

I take my drink and look back at Denise. "The band has been going for a few years. Mostly rock."

"How'd you all meet?" she asks, taking hers. I'm about to answer, but she's distracted by the lemon and rose. "Oh my gosh. This is so pretty." She takes a drink. "It's delicious, too. Good choice, Tom."

I laugh. "To answer your question, we're all fans of the Grateful Dead. I hitched a ride to a concert there a couple summers ago. I was supposed to go with my brother. He bailed on me. But Frank, Donna, and Wally—sorry, my bandmates—were the ones that picked me up."

"The Dead!" she exclaims. "I've never been to one of their shows. Maybe one day."

"There's nothing else like it in the entire world," I say.

"Did they already have the band?" Denise asks. "Sorry, I'm so curious."

I shake my head. "No... so, Frank's from Philly and he met Donna when she was passing through. They're married now."

"No way. How did they meet? Was it love at first sight?" When I don't respond immediately, she adds, "If you want to tell me. I'm sorry. I'm a hopeless romantic. I love love." She smiles, showing her teeth. They're crooked, bent into each other at awkward angles. It's cute, her smile. And she's never let anyone see it. Not ever.

"Well, she was doing caricatures in this park, and he walked by. I think he paused by her stand or something and she said, 'sir, if there's any doubt, you have the perfect face to be carica-tured.' And it happened pretty quickly for them after that. But they tell the story better than I do."

If there was any doubt her teeth were really crooked and I wasn't just hallucinating, it goes away when Denise smiles again. "She's got to do all of you."

"Oh, she has. She makes all of our concert posters," I say. "Maybe one day when we're rich and famous it'll be an album cover. Just like The Doors and how they're all circus performers on the cover of—"

"*Strange Days?*"

As I nod, Denise beams.

"I love that album," she says. "Anyway, train, off the rails. You were telling me how your band got started."

"Well, Frank and Wally were work friends and the three of them hit it off. In '72, they came to Newark. When *I* met them, they'd been trying to put something together for a while and were just looking for a bassist."

"No way," Denise says. "That's fate."

I laugh. "Sure. If you believe in it."

"I know I do," Denise insists.

I give her a look.

"No, really, I do," Denise continues. "There's too many things in this world to just explain away by coincidence or luck."

"Easy to say if you come here with a notebook and a dream, get plucked from obscurity and end up on Ed Sullivan."

Denise's face goes tight, and I worry I've insulted her, especially when she abruptly changes the subject. "Anyways, what's in a name?"

"That which we call a rose," I tease.

"Why are you called The Hermits?" she asks.

"Oh," I say. "Honestly... the four of us are all kind of dorks. We're all like, the black sheep of our families, I guess, and before we found each other we all related to the idea of wanting to be away from everyone and everything."

"I resonate with that," Denise says with a whisper. "Anyways, you guys must really trust each other."

"Yeah," I say. "We do. We live together and everything, so we kind of have to."

"You live together?" Denise says with a laugh.

"Yep. Four of us, plus my girlfriend."

"Girlfriend?" Denise says playfully. "What's her name? Where is she?"

"Patty. She's holding down the fort back in Newark while we're here," I explain.

"Oh," she says. "Is she a Patricia?"

I nod.

"That's *my* middle name. So, I like her already."

I smile.

After she takes another sip of her Sparkle, she inspects the glass carefully. "Have you ever made these at home?"

"No."

"I have to figure out how to do that. It's so good."

I manage a laugh. As my cheeks redden, I can't quite think of what else to say.

"How old are you?"

"Twenty-five," I tell her.

"And your bandmates?"

"Frank's twenty-six, Donna's twenty-three and Wally's twenty-four. Patty's twenty-two. She's an honorary Hermit."

Denise smiles. "You guys are all a year apart? That's cute."

"Yeah."

"Anyway, I guess I'm next in the sequence because I'm twenty-one."

I smile at her.

"So, what brings you to LA?"

"We have an audition at Skylark in two days. To do the new Malone's jingle."

Denise laughs. "You're serious?"

"Yeah," I reply. "Why wouldn't I be?"

"Rupert's working on that with Kathy York. Have you met Kathy?"

"Me? No," I say. "Donna, she's like, our manager too. She's the one that's been talking to Kathy, so."

"Wait," Denise says. "She's also your manager?"

"Well, not officially." I'm red as a tomato as I steal another look back at the hotel doors. I don't know how much longer I can handle this conversation alone.

"So are you guys just in LA for a couple of days?"

"That's the plan," I tell her. "We were kind of talking about maybe seeing if we could get any gigs while we're out here, but who knows. Just taking it one step at a time."

Denise chugs the last of her drink and checks her watch. "I actually should probably go check on Rupert, but." She borrows a pen from the bartender, takes a napkin, scrawls something, and hands it to me.

My House
2202 Percival Lane
Come whenever
(after 8pm! ☺)

My grasp on it is shaky as she explains.

"We're having a party tomorrow night. You should come. It'll be a good chance to meet people. Michael Rooney and Sheila Carlton, I don't know if you like their movies but they'll be there. But come early. They stopped being cool when they had a kid. Joking, obviously, but, they will have to turn in to take care of their little girl."

"Thank you. That's very generous," I manage.

"Of course," she says. "Besides, I need more friends my age. But there'll be a lot of people there. You'll make some good connections. Maybe you could even play the song for us."

"Um," I say with a blush. "Maybe. As long as, with your husband, it's not giving us an unfair advantage or anything."

"I didn't say you had to play the jingle," Denise says. "And besides. The universe wanted us to meet. Not anyone else. You shouldn't be ashamed of that."

"Right," I reply.

"Anyways." Denise stands up, gets the bartender's attention, and closes out the tab. "Maybe see you tomorrow, Tom?"

"Yeah, of course," I say.

She beams a smile at me. It takes until she walks out of my line of sight for my jaw to drop.

"So, she was just, right there, and started talking to you?" Frank exclaims for the fifth time, once we're all settled in the suite. I sit on the couch with Wally as Donna sits on the chair and Frank stands beside her.

"Her husband too," I say.

"Shit," Frank says. "I can't believe you met Rupert Morris. Did you say anything about who we were?"

"I didn't get the chance before Denise showed up." I reach

into my pocket and show them the note. "Tomorrow night. She invited us."

Donna takes it in her hands as Wally and Frank bend over to look. "Tom, you're not pulling our legs, are you?" she finally says.

"Definitely not. And Donna, I told her about the doppelgänger thing. She wants to meet you."

"Oh, jeez, okay." Donna sets the note down on the coffee table and takes a moment to catch her breath.

"We're going, right?" I ask them.

"Of course we're going," Donna says.

"That's what I thought," I remark.

"Are we going to have time to work on the song? A bunch of record people are going to be there, aren't they?" Wally asks.

"Michael Rooney and Sheila Carlton, too," I tell him. "Maybe he can sign your book."

"No way," Wally says. "Alrighty then."

"We got this," Frank reassures him. He finds an open spot on the floor. "By the way, anyone think of any ideas?"

"I did," I say after a beat. "Well, not musically, necessarily, but conceptually."

"Okay. Tell us more," Frank says.

I take a deep breath, thinking once again of that afternoon with Rick and the bike. "Well, it could be something like... Malone's brings people together. It gives them happy memories. It gives them a feeling that everything is going to be okay."

"Holy shit, Thomas, since when did you become a capitalist?"

I laugh. "First of all, please don't call me Thomas. Second, I'm just throwing out ideas."

"No, it's good," he says. He takes his guitar out of its case behind him, holding his pick in between his teeth as he gets it in tune. "Something like..."

He strums a few notes before I realize it's just the start of "This Land Is Your Land."

"Hey," I say. "That's taken."

Frank addresses the room. "They didn't say anything about doing a riff on something, did they?" His grin is goofy and mischievous.

"How many times do I have to tell you that you're not and will never be Pete Seeger?"

As Frank starts singing "You Are My Sunshine" off-key. Wally stifles a laugh, and a moment later, Donna does the same. So do I.

I know that we're about to make something special. We're getting in sync. This is just the way we do it. And we don't have to say words for Wally to get his drumsticks and for Donna to unpack her keys. Finally, I do the same with my bass. It doesn't take long for the rest of the world to fall away.

six

I visit the Providence Civic Center again in my dreams. It's a beautiful summer day, just like last time, but now, Jack's beside me. He glows in exactly the way he did in high school, before the world got the better of us.

"I hear the girls go crazy for this guy," Jack says with a grin as we approach the crowd. There's even more girls than there were last time.

"So, why are we here again?" I say.

"Because, we gotta know what we're doing wrong," he replies.

"Speak for yourself," I shoot back. I see Patty there, in the crowd, her eyes distant. She's as beautiful as ever. "Excuse me," I tell Jack.

He obliges and I approach her.

"Took you long enough," Patty says.

"What do you mean?" I ask, confused.

"I didn't think you'd ever show up," she says, taking my hands in hers. "It's too bad you can't stay for the show."

"What do you mean? Of course I can."

I don't get an answer, but the image of her sad face freezes in my mind.

I WAKE at six in the morning to another cold sweat just as Donna's gotten up to make coffee.

As we sit, wait for the coffee to percolate and for the others to wake up, I tell her about the two dreams, and how similar they were.

"Does it count as recurring if I've had it twice?" I ask her.

"If it stayed with you, then sure," she says. "Who's the musician that you're waiting to see?"

"That's the thing, I don't know," I say. "Only that I'm drawn to him and I don't know why, because his target audience isn't... me?"

Donna's eyes widen. "You know what I think this is?"

"What?"

"Well, you'll have to let me know if you have it again, because it'll mean that something is still unresolved, but I think it means that success isn't going to look like how you imagined it."

"Like writing a jingle for Malone's?" I say.

She nods. "Sure, like that."

I rub my eyes. "Jack was so clear to me. I know none of you ever met him, but... the fact that he couldn't get around the damn draft. You know, in January it will have been six years since he died?"

"I know," Donna whispers.

"I think about him all the time. I'm never going to be the person I was before it happened."

"What do you mean?" Donna asks.

I can't put the feeling into words, but I only know it has to do with him being there one minute and gone the next. So, I sniffle and say, "I think I'm having buyer's remorse for this hotel room. Make me feel like I'm not crazy, please."

"You're not crazy," Donna tells me. "By the way, I'm glad we're here."

ONCE THE OTHERS GET UP, we stall for as long as possible before we're forced to comply with our noon checkout time. If nothing else, the song is in a much better place than it was the night before. It's still not ready for the audition. It's definitely not in any sort of place to show people we might have to impress at Denise's party.

We were just about ready to accept and make do with the circumstances when reality hits us like an anvil to the head.

We walk into the Eagle Rock hotel to find that the lights are all off. At first, I think that maybe they're trying to save on the electric bill. I wouldn't put it past this place. The front desk lady's eyeing us. As we keep walking, she keeps staring and I think she's probably bored. We get about halfway to the hallway when she clears her throat. I return her gaze first.

"Hey, folks," she says with a plastered smile.

We all stop. "Hello," I reply.

"Just so you folks know, the power's out in the building," she says. "Somebody's coming to fix it as soon as possible. Apologies for the inconvenience." I look at her and see the fear in her face.

I nod vaguely and look back at the others, who all offer a collective shrug.

"Hey," Donna says with a grin. "Forces us to work more on the song, right?"

"Well, that's going to be a little challenging without being able to plug our gear in, right?" Frank says wryly.

"You have your acoustic, don't you?" Donna says.

"Last I checked."

The front desk lady watches us, looking like a deer in headlights. She seems relieved that we didn't just blow a gasket. I wave and gesture the others forward.

As we're all sitting in Frank and Donna's room, we've hit a wall. The song is supposed to be thirty seconds, and we only have the first ten. Even then, it might be complete shit. We have no idea and won't until we get away from it. We've had to work through regular interruptions from screaming children and loud talkers. The highlight was two people who thought it would be a great idea to have a twenty-five-minute-long conversation about God knows what—it seemed like gossip about a mutual friend from the bits I was able to pick up—right outside our door.

Still, Donna wants to keep going, and Frank wants us to get fresh air.

They've been going in circles for the last five minutes. I know because I checked my watch when the fight started and have been timing it ever since. Donna stands behind her keyboard and Frank is beside her. Wally and I have migrated to the extra bed as we occasionally give one another uncomfortable glances.

They don't fight often, but Donna's anxiety and Frank's

tendency to avoid conflict can be a bad combination when both are under stress. Like right now.

"We have limited time, Jesus. I won't be able to properly enjoy myself if we go out," Donna says.

"Sweetheart, we're just going to get more frustrated the longer we stay in this hotel room," Frank reasons. "Come on! We're in LA. There's so much to see."

"We can see stuff after the audition," Donna says. "Besides, we were just at the Chateau yesterday."

"Where we worked on the song all day and night," Frank replies.

Wally clears his throat. "I think Frank might have a point. We can come at it fresh tomorrow."

Donna sighs. "Great. Taking his side like you always do."

Frank scoffs. "We're just having a discussion. You're the one that's making it into a big deal."

"Hey," I cut in. "Can you two not, please?" My mind's wandered to the time they took a "break" a year and a half ago. Even though Frank ended up winning her back with his own recording of Ritchie Valens's "Donna," and they got married a few months afterwards, I would really rather we didn't repeat that whole chapter.

Everyone looks in my direction.

"What do you want to do, Tom?" Donna asks.

"I, personally, would like to explore a bit more of the city," I say. "Who knows, maybe the party tonight will spur some inspiration for us."

"Okay," Donna says. "Just reminding everyone that we're out here no thanks to any of you."

Frank raises his eyebrow. "What's that supposed to mean?"

"Guys, seriously, save it," I snap.

Just then, there's a knock at the door. I stand up to go and answer it.

It's a staff member. He's young. Our age at most. "Hey folks, how are you doing?" he says.

"Fine," I say, wondering in the back of my mind if there's another issue with the electricity or something else in the building.

"Just wanted to pass on that there's a been a couple of noise complaints. I'm not sure what's going on in here, but please try to be mindful of the other guests, alright?"

I scoff. "Would you like to tell that to the parents who let their children run wild in this hotel?"

"We haven't gotten any complaints about that," the staff member says. "Only this room."

I see the look in his eyes and feel bad about raising my voice. "You're just doing your job," I reassure him. "We'll keep it down."

"Appreciate it, folks," he says, scurrying off.

I close the door and sit back down on the bed. "We're all under stress, but let's please, not fight. Skylark, no Skylark, I want to have a good time here." If I'd wanted to add fuel to the fire, I could have challenged Donna on her comment since, so far, I've funded almost this entire thing. But I don't want to have conflict with any of my bandmates when it's so obviously coming from external sources.

"Sure, let's go out," Donna says. "What did we have in mind?"

As they discuss, I realize with a start that I haven't called Patty since we've gotten here. I rush to the phone, thinking I'm about to be in the doghouse myself, especially once she finds out how much money I spent on the Chateau Marmont.

It rings four times. I'm about to hang up when I hear her voice.

"This is Patty."

"Hey, Patty-cake," I say, my heart racing.

"Tom," she replies. "Is everything okay? How's LA?"

"Good. Busy. I'm sorry I haven't called."

"No problem," she says. "I figured you were busy."

"How's Diane?"

"Fine."

The Chateau can wait. "How's the house?"

Patty laughs. "It's missing all of you. And especially one Tom Hargrove."

"Who is about to take his first steps into the Twilight Zone," I reply in my best Rod Serling impression.

She laughs again. "That sounded ominous." I try to picture the dimples on her face, her freckles, and her beautiful blue eyes. I miss her so much.

"Do you consider a party at Denise Peck's house 'the Twilight Zone?'"

"Excuse me?" Patty says.

"I'll tell you more later. Love you." I quickly hang up. I don't want to fight with her, and I'm sure that I will if I tell her about the Chateau.

Everyone's looking in my direction.

"We were thinking of going to the Walk of Fame and maybe down to the beach if we have time before Denise's," Donna says.

"Sounds like a plan," I tell them.

seven

"Okay, Paul McCartney," Jack said as I set his bass aside.

"I get it, you want to be the lead," I said. "No need to flatter me." It was 1967. Fall. Outside, the leaves had started to change colors, but it was still warm and sunny.

Jack took his guitar and sang the first few lines of "I'm Only Sleeping."

I picked up his bass again and followed in sync. Something about this felt good. By the end of the song, we were both smiling.

"So, Tom, when are we going to make this official?" Jack said.

I looked at him.

"The band."

Wondering what Mom and Dad would think, I gave a hesitant laugh.

Jack read my mind. "Come on. Your folks had to have known when they signed you up for those lessons years ago."

I sighed. "I don't think they were thinking too deep on it, to be honest."

"You *are* a musician, Tom Hargrove," he said. "And it would be an honor to do this with you."

"TOM." Donna gets my attention as we wind through the Sunset Strip. We're on the bus, about to reach our stop.

"Sorry," I mutter.

She just smiles at me.

As we get off and start to climb up the windy hills, it hits me that over half of my savings has disappeared in about a week and a half. It all started with Jack. As much as I loved my music lessons growing up, I wouldn't have done anything with it if not for him.

Would my life be different if he'd never pushed me in this direction?

Would it be better?

My life changed that day in more ways than one, too. Cindy had come down the steps of the basement, reminding Jack he'd promised to walk with her to gymnastics class.

"I'm leaving anyway," I'd said before he had a chance to respond. "I can walk with you, Cindy."

Cindy looked at me, and then at her brother. Her class was at the Newark Community Center, about five blocks out of the way, and all of us knew it. "Sure, that's fine," she said. "As long as you don't forget to pick me up, big bro."

"Oh, sure," Jack groaned.

Once we were outside, Cindy confessed, "My parents don't want me to walk anywhere alone. Which is dumb, because I'm not a kid anymore. I can't wait to get my driver's license."

"I'll have mine soon," I told her with a smile.

"Anyways," Cindy said. "I heard you and Jack are going to start a band?"

"I guess," I said, laughing. He'd been planning this for a while, apparently.

"You should call yourselves Abbott and Costello."

She saw my pale expression and blushed bright red. "I'm sorry. I meant that as a compliment."

I laughed, too. "It's okay. Who's Abbott and who's Costello?"

I don't remember what she said.

WALKING into Laurel Canyon brings me back to the present. We'd spent the afternoon in Hollywood—looking at the footprints outside of Grauman's as we navigated a line of people waiting to see *Star Wars* for the millionth time was a highlight —but I didn't feel much. It was all manufactured. Not like this. This is real. No one's putting on a face or trying to present anything to anyone. They're just out here, living their lives.

Walking past the houses, they're all different, all uniquely expressive of whoever lives there. I see some with the lights on and wonder who these people are and what they must be up to. I think of what it must have been like not quite ten years ago, with John and Michelle Phillips, Jim Morrison, and so many more writing music about this place.

It's a nice change of pace from the cookie-cutter houses all over Newark, where the only difference is in the color of the roofs and picket fences. There's one I like that's all in white, from the roof to the panels to the doors and the shutters.

"Making us get our workout in!" Frank teases as we traverse

a particularly steep hill. I catch the smile he and Donna exchange as he takes her hand to steady her. They seem like they've made up, but something tells me we're still skating on thin ice. Since we're smack in the middle of our stress, I know it won't take much for them to break. All I can do is keep the levity the best I can.

"I like this one," I tell Wally, who's walking beside me.

"A little too much white," Wally says.

I get Donna and Frank's attention. "Verdict on the white house?"

"I'm a fan," says Donna. She turns to Frank. "Let's move in here one day."

"You got it, honey," Frank says.

I'm in rarified air. I can't explain it, but suddenly everything else, all the stressors waiting for me back home, wash away. None of it matters.

About halfway up our trek, we pass the Canyon Country Store.

We're on Love Street, standing right out front of the store where the creatures meet. I know it's just a convenience store and we have no reason to go inside, but I can't help but stop and gape.

I saw Jim Morrison in 1968, and he was about the size of a pin from the very back row of the auditorium. Beforehand, I only saw him as the Lizard King, a poet and a performer with a perfect life and effortless cool. Now, picturing him here, taking it all in, comes easily to me.

"You okay, Tom?" Donna finally asks.

"Yeah," I say. "It's just, everything suddenly makes sense."

. . .

WHILE I CAN'T SAY I ever spent much time imagining what Denise's place must be like, the house on Percival Lane fits her perfectly. Even its positioning—atop a long steep hill at the end of the cul-de-sac—is symbolic. It's just after nine when we approach the gate. This tall, imposing house, with its wood walls and floor-to-ceiling windows is a log cabin with the shape and position of a fairytale castle. It's a retreat away from the hustle of LA from within the city itself.

We walk past a low stone fence onto the property itself. We hear music coming from inside. Each of us exchanges glances and takes a deep breath.

We see a built, blond man alongside a woman with long, dark hair leaving out the door. I realize it's Michael Rooney and Sheila Carlton about a second before Denise trails behind them. They're talking about something. I'm thinking about how on earth we're going to come into this conversation when Denise sees us.

"You made it!" she exclaims. I see her outfit fully now. It's a silver sequined dress, and she's got the makeup to match. "Mike, Sheila, meet new people!"

Their eyes turn to us. I look over at Wally. Color drains from his face in an instant as Denise ushers us forward.

A second later we're introducing ourselves to Michael Rooney and Sheila Carlton.

"No relation to Mickey," Michael jokes, his voice commanding.

"Who's Mickey Rooney?" Frank teases.

"Tom and his bandmates are from Newark, New Jersey," Denise announces. She notices Donna then. "Are you my twin?"

Donna's face is beet red. "I guess so." Denise approaches Donna and the two start chatting.

"It's like looking in a mirror," Michael says of the two.

Frank smiles wryly. "Donna gets told she looks like Denise a lot."

Michael notices Wally then and extends his hand. "I didn't catch your name."

"Wally," he mutters. "I love your work. You're an inspiration to me."

Michael laughs and turns to Sheila. "Well, someone's paying attention, right?"

"You two headed off?" I say.

Sheila nods. "We have to make sure our daughter hasn't driven the sitter mad." I'm not around British people often, but when I am, I'm always amazed by how elegant they sound.

"How old's your daughter?" I ask as Donna and Denise turn back to join the circle.

"Joan just turned four," Michael says with a dry smile.

"And already following in her parents' footsteps?" Denise says with a grin.

"She was a star in our church's Christmas pageant last year," Sheila tells us.

"Rupert saw it," Denise says. "He told me that girl's got a future."

"Yeah," Michael says wryly. He puts his hand on Sheila's back and leads her forward. "Have a good night, all."

Just like that, they're gone.

We hesitate at the door for a moment before Denise ushers us in. I end up walking alongside Denise, noticing her dress again.

She sees me looking and smiles.

"I like the dress," I say.

"Thanks," Denise says. "I don't look like a prostitute?"

"No," I say. "I was actually thinking that you look like Daisy Buchanan."

Denise blushes. "This dress is from 1925, you know. It's one of my favorites. But Rupert thinks it makes me look like a prostitute."

I don't reply.

"Anyways, he's not here."

"Oh? Where is he?"

By then, we've entered her house and are met with wood-paneled walls and plush, red carpeting. It's overwhelmed by the potent scent of alcohol, marijuana, and incense. At the end of the hallways straight ahead of us is a breathtaking view of the city below.

"New York," Denise says, answering my question. She sees Donna, Frank, and Wally lingering at the edge of the hallway. "Come on, guys! Don't be shy!"

There's a group of people sitting on the sofa around Mila Potter. They're all smoking grass. Her long, brown hair falls to her back, perfectly framing her light-brown skin. Her red-and-blue dress is stunning, and she looks like she's walked right off the covers of any of the magazines she's graced over the years. Of course Denise knows Mila.

All of us are still frozen in place when Mila looks up and catches eyes with Donna. "Hello, friend!" she exclaims. "Come get a light?"

Donna follows, and so do Frank and Wally. I hear Mila say, "Santos, is that—"

"Filipino," Frank says with a smile.

"Do you have family there?"

"Grandparents," says Frank, putting his hand on Donna's shoulder. "They haven't met her yet, but we're saving so we can go and visit."

I'm still left with Denise in the hallway as they talk. I look back and smile at her. "Hey, I want to show you something."

It's the lowest floor—"the closest thing she'll have to a basement up here"—built right into the edge of the hill.

"Does Rupert go away a lot?" I ask as we descend the stairs.

"Yeah," she says. "Work takes him all over. But that's okay."

"I meant to ask, how do you know Michael and Sheila?"

"Oh!" Denise exclaims. "You saw *The Edge of Eden*, right? The movie they did together?"

"I sure have," I say tiredly. That had been a date night with Cindy. She'd been in a bad mood that day and had refused to talk to me after the movie. I don't even remember why.

"When they pass by the girl that's singing 'Johnny Appleseed?' The farmer's daughter?" Denise proudly points to herself, and I blink in faint recognition.

"That's right," I say. "How old were you?"

"Fifteen," she replies. "I had my album out by then, but no one knew who I was. Ed Sullivan was later that year and the rest is history."

We get closer to the door, and she opens it with a smile.

The walls are painted in orange and covered with a mix of old records, art, and movie posters.

"You want to hear Queen's new single?" she says.

I process on a delay. "What?"

"I mean, do you want to hear their new single that's

coming out next month? Rupert stole it from Elektra. Before he moved over to Skylark."

I eagerly nod. She gets the record out of its sleeve from beside the player.

She puts it in and moves the needle to the center. It's upbeat. We will rock you? There's no mistaking their distinct sound, but it's unlike anything they've ever done.

Denise starts clapping her hands and stomping her feet in rhythm with the song.

We sit there, just listening until the song ends and Denise has to flip the record over. It's replaced with a slower, but just as majestic proclamation about being a champion of the world. Listening to this, I can't help but feel like what we've been trying to write is complete shit. Crayon drawings. This is real music.

"Who's your favorite artist?" Denise asks.

I pause. "That's like asking me to pick a favorite child."

"Who's the first one that comes to mind? Don't overthink it," Denise says, smiling. "I won't be offended if you exclude present company."

"The Grateful Dead," I say.

She chuckles. "Of course. I remember." She moves her legs up onto the couch, kneeling forward and leaning in to face me. I smell her perfume then. I don't quite recognize the scent, only that it's floral and sweet. "They just had the most-attended concert of all time. At least, here in the States. Ticketed, anyway."

"Wait, really?" I ask.

"Yeah, in New Jersey. Rupert was telling me," Denise explains. "Just under a hundred and ten thousand people, I think."

It hits me. "Englishtown, right? I was there."

Her mouth widens. "No way! Just recently, too. Was it amazing?"

I nod. Of course the Dead were the ones to do it. And here we are staking everything for a thirty-second jingle for Malone's.

"So, what is it about them?" she asks me with a smirk. "The Dead, I mean."

"I wouldn't be here tonight," I explain. "In so many ways."

"Would you call yourself a Deadhead?"

I nod.

"Let's take it a step further," Denise says. "Who's your favorite member of the Grateful Dead?"

"Cliché, but Garcia," I say with a laugh. "If you're going to ask me why, I'd say he's got a great story. I've seen him four times and he's always super fun."

"Only four times?" Denise teases. "That's weak by Dead-head standards."

I shrug.

"I'm getting to my point, I promise," Denise continues. "What is it about the Grateful Dead that makes you want to follow them around from place to place to hear the same songs?"

"Wouldn't you know?" I ask.

"What do you mean?" she replies, giving me a blank stare.

"Why do people follow *you* from place to place?"

"Hell if I know," she mutters. "It's just..."

"It's just what?" I've noticed I've leaned in closer. My posture matches hers. I smell her perfume more strongly now.

Her brown eyes are watery, almost like she's about to cry. "I hear music like this and I think nobody cares about me and my stupid love songs."

I raise my eyebrow, disbelieving. "That's impossible. And your songs aren't stupid."

"According to Rupert, they're for little girls." Denise says, sniffling. "I have so many ideas, Tom. I have like, three note-books full of songs and he won't let me. He says—"

"Wait a minute. Why does Rupert have any say in your career? Hasn't he not been your manager for—"

"Three years," Denise says dryly. "Why do you think he left Elektra? So he can keep an eye on me. Put down my music and make sure it's all I ever play."

"Oh," I say quietly. "Sounds like he's got you between a rock and a hard place."

Denise shrugs. "I was just curious about your experience because I go on tour and when I'm standing on stage I can't even see their faces. It's not like the early days. Where's the connection? How do I connect with people?"

"Denise," I say. "You sold out Michigan Stadium. I don't know what you're talking about."

She sniffles again, blinking back tears. "Anyways, what is it about the Grateful Dead?"

I pause to think. It's a good question. No one's ever asked me before, and I've never stopped to reflect. "The community that they build with their music, I would say. The way they make me feel like everything's going to be okay. Think about the band itself. They're seven people from different walks of life, different musical styles. They get on stage, you don't know where it's going to lead, but they get in sync and something magical happens."

She nods slowly.

71

"It just works," I add.

Denise turns her gaze away from me then. "You want acid?"

"I sure do," I reply. She gets two tabs from inside a drawer beside her.

We let them dissolve on our tongues. As she smiles at me and I smile back, I eagerly wait for the rest of the world to fall away.

I HAVEN'T HAD a trip this strong since I was still with Cindy.

The entire room and its surroundings go black and white, like I'm in an old episode of *I Love Lucy,* complete with TV static to match.

Denise is at least five times my size, towering over me as I feel like I'm about to fade into nothingness.

I don't remember much else, but I hear Cindy's voice, telling me that I'm impossible to be around. That I overcomplicate things.

Then everything fades.

I wake up in a sweat, still lying on the couch. I realize a moment later my head is on Denise's lap, and that her hand is on my shoulder. She's still passed out.

I sit up with a start, and she wakes up too.

I notice the clock. It's four-thirty in the morning. My head instantly throbs in pain, As I rub my temples, I try not to think of why I was lying on her lap.

"Who's Cindy? And Jack?" Denise asks. "You were talking about them a lot."

"Don't worry about it," I mutter. I manage my way to a stand and work my way up the stairs.

The crowd's thinned, but I notice Mila, Donna, Wally, and Frank. They're sitting on the floor around the table where I left them and smoking a fresh joint.

Donna sees me. "There you are! Come join!"

I wearily make my way over to a sit.

"Do you want a drink, Tom?" Donna asks. "The night is young!"

"It's four-thirty in the morning," I say tiredly.

"Where'd you run off to?" Frank asks.

"Doesn't matter," I say.

Frank raises his eyebrow. Donna gets my attention and turns to Mila. "This is Tom. Our bassist."

"Nice to meet you, Tom," says Mila.

"My girlfriend loves you," I tell her.

Mila smiles slightly. "Where is she tonight?"

"Home in New Jersey," I explain. "She's bought your clothes before." My face tightens as I think about the cutoffs incident. Thank God Patty was finally able to get the stain out.

Mila just blushes.

"Mila's brother runs the Ivy Room and they said they're looking for a new act starting a week from Monday. And guess what? It's in Eagle Rock, where we're staying," Donna explains.

"It'd be twice a week, but maybe something to get you on your feet," Mila says. "Since you've come all the way out here."

I take a deep breath. Our gigs have always been one and done things. Every time we're lucky enough to secure one, it's over, and then it's back to busting our asses. We've never had anything like this back in Newark.

I nod, taking in what she's saying. "You haven't even heard us play yet. Are you sure?"

"You wouldn't be here tonight if you weren't worth it," Mila says with a smile. "To be clear, you'll have to audition for my brother, but it'll be a formality after I put in the word. Besides, I have a good feeling and my intuition has never led me astray."

"Oh?" I ask.

"My spiritual guides told me that I'd be taking on a mentorship role," Mila says. "They specifically told me they saw a group of four."

After a beat, Donna leads forward. "Did your spiritual guides say anything about the future of this group of four?"

"No," Mila replies. "That's still unclear."

We all exchange a look.

"Do any of you meditate? It's a great way to clear the mind," Mila says.

"I've tried," Donna says. "But it's hard for me to focus."

I have. Cindy and I went to this little place in Newark once a week before drugs became our meditation. Ever since we broke up, I haven't touched anything New Age. I don't want to get into that in front of everyone else, so I don't say anything.

"You should all come to the class I take tomorrow evening," she says. "It's close to the beach. It's a great way to unwind."

"That's very generous," Wally tells her. "Thank you."

We're distracted by Denise coming up the stairs. She stops, looks at me, and then makes a beeline for the back patio. Mila sees this too, writes her number on a slip of paper and hands it to Donna. Then she gets up and joins Denise outside.

Donna's pants lack pockets, so she puts the paper into one of Frank's. He turns to me. "Is that where you were?"

I play dumb. "What?"

"Downstairs, with Denise?"

"It wasn't like that," I manage.

"Then why's your face bright red?" he asks.

Donna opens her mouth and takes a breath.

I raise my eyebrows at her.

"You know what, never mind," she says.

I give her a look, which she ignores.

A millisecond later, I catch eyes with Frank. "Tom, can I speak with you?" he says.

I nod and follow him out the front door.

"What? What did I do?" I ask once we're outside.

He sighs. "Nothing, it's just obvious that she's into you."

"Who? Denise? You've got to be kidding me."

"Donna and Wally noticed it too. What did you do down in her basement?"

I feel like I'm on trial. "Nothing. We just tripped."

He gives me a disbelieving look, and the tenseness in my body grows.

"I hope you're not insinuating what I think you are, because—"

"The only one who's insinuating things is you, Tom! Should I be worried?"

"No!" I exclaim. "Absolutely not! Where is this coming from anyways?"

Frank doesn't answer the question. "Clearly, you're getting special treatment."

"And?"

Frank says nothing.

I give him a look.

He still doesn't say anything.

"Come on, spit it out!" I yell.

"Just be careful, man."

I'm getting angrier by the second. "You're not my dad, so fuck off!"

"I'm going back in. You can stay or go."

I hesitate. I wait for Frank to go back inside, and then I start walking.

eight

It's a solid twenty-five-minute walk to where the bus let us off on Sunset Boulevard. By the time I get there, I find out the bus isn't running this early. For another twenty-five minutes, I try and fail to hitch a ride. I give up and spend ten bucks on a cab. Another chunk of my savings is gone just like that.

It's daylight by the time I'm back at the hotel. I already want to make up with Frank, but I'm hoping he apologizes to me too. Yeah, it was a jerk move of me to ditch them at the party, but there's nothing going on between me and Denise anyway. Even if I somehow ended up lying in her lap, so what? We're both spoken for.

Still, I call Patty as soon as I get to the room. I need to hear her voice and remind myself that even though she's on the other side of the country, she's the only one for me.

She doesn't answer. She must be at work or with Diane. *Figures.*

I flop onto my bed, only to be woken up at just after eight in the morning when I hear Wally come back.

"Hey," I say.

"We ate on the way back, so you're on your own for breakfast, but I'm about to crash," he says.

"Is Frank still mad?"

Wally shrugs. "You two work it out, okay?"

"Sure."

I promptly fall back to sleep.

IT'S ALMOST eleven by the time I wake up again, and I'm starving. Wally's still passed out as I change my clothes, grab my wallet, and plan to go across the street to a donut shop.

I almost make it down the hallway when I hear Frank's voice. "Hey, Tom, wait up."

I stop, turn around and sigh as he catches up with me. "How was the rest of the party?" I ask.

He shrugs. "It was fine. Mila's going to talk to her brother about having us audition if we're cool staying in LA for at least a month. Maybe longer."

Processing this, I look ahead and then back at Frank. I tell him about my plans to get donuts.

"I'll come with," he says.

"Cool."

"I'm sorry for being such an asshole," Frank says. "It's just, Denise—"

"What?"

"It's obvious how she feels about you, man."

"Please drop it," I say. "Besides, it's not like we're ever going to see her again."

"Okay," Frank says.

We exit the hotel then.

"I owe you an apology for comparing you to my dad," I say as we cross the street. "That was low."

"Hey," Frank says, patting my shoulder. "Don't worry about it. You gonna come to Mila's thing tonight?"

"Her meditation group?" I ask. I'm surprised that I remember through the fog of everything else.

"Yeah," he says. "She said she'll pick us up from the hotel at six thirty."

"Are we going to have time to finish the song?" I ask.

"Yeah. We'll work on it as much as we can and if we still need time we'll do more when we get back."

"Okay." I wonder if spending more time away from the reason we're here is really the decision we should be making right now, but Ivy's and the connection with Mila is worth something too. Besides, we're going to get to a point where we're as ready for the audition as we'll ever be.

Since Donna and Wally are still sleeping, we end up eating the donuts there. It's a worn-down, cramped space with harsh fluorescent lighting that's seen better days. It's hard to relax as people keep coming in and out of the door right beside us.

The focus of the conversation shifts to Ivy's. It's nice, for once, to not think about the jingle.

"I mean, if we stay, what are we going to do about a place to live?" I ask.

"Well, we'd make a hundred and fifty a week," Frank says. "Split four ways, it's not great money, but it's something."

"And how long would it last?" I ask.

"At least a month. Maybe more if we keep at it."

"A month is a long time to be gone, you know," I say.

"I know, it's just..." Frank rubs his eyes. "This is more than we ever got back home, right?"

"Right," I say.

"I think we should seriously think about it," he says. "Come on, it's *Mila Potter*. This could lead to something even better than Malone's."

"I agree. Let's think about it."

"You sound hesitant," Frank says.

"Let's get through Malone's first and see if we can even afford to stay," I say. I'm thinking about the money in my savings, and I know he is too.

"Fair enough," he replies.

THAT AFTERNOON, once we're all back at the hotel, we make a field trip to the Malone's in Sherman Oaks. We only find out it's there after probing it out of the same front desk lady who told us about the power outage.

This one is twice as big as the one in Newark and spread out across three floors.

As we walk in the revolving doors, the cursive, blue sign on the opposite wall immediately draws attention to itself. As does, of all things, Denise's face. The perfume ad she models for takes up an entire endcap display. Her brown eyes, her sultry stare draw me in even through the ad's hazy filter, like I'll be drawn into the photoshoot if I take another step forward.

Frank sees me looking and gives me a glare, which I shrug off as we keep walking. It's not a second before Denise's voice fills the store. "Blue Roses," the title track of her debut album, was the first song of hers I ever heard. It follows us as a stark reminder that there's no escaping whatever's happening to us now.

We wander aimlessly for a while, not saying anything, just

taking it all in, if there is even anything deeper to glean. I can't remember the last time I've been in a Malone's, but something about it feels oddly sterile. We make our way past the home goods and go to the second floor, where they have clothes.

Once we get off the escalator, Donna is instantly drawn to a long, blue dress with gold floral stitching. She takes it off the hanger and twirls around.

"And the Grammy goes to... The Hermits!" she exclaims.

Frank gives her a look as Denise's song ends and is broken by a soft announcer's voice. "Attention, Malone's shoppers. This is a reminder to please have your payment method ready upon checkout. We accept cash, check, American Express..."

I tune out the voice as Donna wordlessly gives up on the fantasy and rejoins us in the aisle.

I hear the announcer say "we thank you for shopping with us" as the radio shifts again. This time, to Queen. "Killer Queen." I try not to think about their new single or how this song can't help but make me think of Denise.

Just be in the moment, I tell myself. I do my best to follow my own advice over the next forty minutes as we traverse through each one of the three floors. But we don't end up buying anything. In fact, we're not really sure if the trip did anything for us or the song in the long run.

But we get back to the hotel just as it's about to start raining, so we have nothing to do but sit and practice until we wait for Mila to come pick us up.

Once we're all in Frank and Donna's room, I try calling the house again. No answer. Patty did say she'd be at Diane's as much as possible.

When I call, Gracie ends up answering. She tells me that

Diane and Patty are out getting dinner, and she's just finished up with a client.

"How's Diane doing?" I ask her.

"Really well, actually," Gracie says. "Just trying to stay busy. That's all we can do right now, right?"

"Tell Patty to call me when she can, please," I say.

"Got it," Gracie replies. I'm about to hang up the phone when she says, "Wait, Tom, while I have you."

I wait.

"Diane was going to try to get a hold of you to see if you still wanted the job at the hospital."

"Oh—" I start, looking back at Wally. "Well, I don't know when we're going to be back."

"I just think she might end up having to go with someone else... you know what, never mind. I'll have her get in touch whether through Patty or whatever's easiest. Anyway, have a good night."

"Night, Gracie." I hang up the phone and face my bandmates.

"What was that about?" Donna asks.

"Wondering if I'm going to take that hospital job in Manhattan, I guess," I say. "I don't want to think about it right now."

"Are you sure?" Frank asks.

"Yes. Let's get this thing ready for tomorrow." I look at the clock. It's 4:30. By 6:15, miraculously, we have thirty seconds of something. I don't know what, exactly, but meditating should be the answer we need.

nine

It's still raining by the time we get down to the lobby.

"Mila never told us what kind of car she drives," Donna says with a dry laugh. "Whoops."

We stand there awkwardly for a few minutes. By 6:37, I'm wondering if she forgot when a cream Mercedes appears in the rain, its top up. Mila waves at us and we all file into the car. Donna takes the front and the rest of us sit in the back. As I sink into the leather seats, I think about how nice it will be to finally have a car again.

"Sorry I'm late," Mila says. "People drive like absolute lunatics in the rain."

"We're from Jersey, so we know," Donna says.

"That's right. Newark."

"Hey, we gave the world Frank Sinatra," I tell Mila.

"Isn't he from Hoboken?" Mila asks.

My face flushes. "It's all the same. Watching the lights of New York City from just over the river. Dreaming of something more."

"You're very poetic, Tom," Mila says.

I blush. That's not something I've ever heard before.

"I remember the feeling when I was a girl. My father was Afro-Swede. My brother and I were the only Afro-Swede children in the whole school. And I thought, one day, we would live in America and never have any problems."

"It's worked out alright for you," Frank tells her.

"Yes," she says. "It has."

"How'd you meet Denise?" I ask.

"Oh, she is such a doll, isn't she?" Mila remarks. "Paris Fashion Week. Two years ago. That was such a lovely time, with lovely people. She and Rupert were there, attending. Of course, all of the designers were vying for her attention."

I nod, thinking of Denise there with the context of what she told me at the party. I picture her drowning in a fur coat, looking beautiful but feeling so alone.

We drive in silence for a while. I watch the rain stream down the window and out at the misty city that surrounds us.

"You know," Mila says, "that rain represents cleansing? Rebirth? Renewal?"

I nod vaguely, and so does everyone else.

"I think it's a beautiful omen for your audition tomorrow," Mila tells us.

"I hope so," Donna whispers.

"No matter what happens," Mila says. "You've come all the way out here for your dream, which is a step that so many never take. That's why I want to help you however I can."

"Thank you," I tell her.

Mila just smiles.

. . .

84

NIGHT'S FALLEN by the time we get to Venice Beach. We pass the houses and beachside storefronts at the heart of town and drive up a windy, hillside road. Even in the darkness, the view is beautiful. We pass a statue of the Buddha and come up on a temple that looks like it belongs to another world.

"What is this place?" Donna asks as we park.

"My lifeline," Mila replies. "I'll cover you all tonight."

"Thank you," Donna says.

As we exit the car, I inhale the scent of rain, ocean, and night air. We might as well have left the real world behind. There's nothing else but peace.

The feeling is even stronger as we enter the simple hallway. I hear the trickle of a water fountain built into the wall as Mila writes a check and leaves it in a desk. I think to ask how much the cover charge is, but I hold off, realizing that I don't want to know.

"It's nonsecular," Mila says. "All faiths are welcome."

"Including atheists?" I ask.

Everyone laughs, including Mila. "Yes," she tells me.

We enter a room with plush, red carpet, accented with gold. Equally nice pillows have been laid out across the floor. The lighting is dim from the glow of candles, and the teacher, an older woman with long gray hair, sits on a chair. There's a few others here.

As I find a seat, a rush of thoughts hit me: I've really spent thousands of dollars of my own money to be here. I really met Denise Peck and tripped with her at a party at her house while my bandmates cozied up to Mila Potter. Now we're here. Tomorrow, we audition. After that, who knows? I can't help but feel like another shoe's going to drop soon. We've been too lucky since we've been here for it not to.

The teacher hits a gong, signaling the start of the session.

I close my eyes and take a deep breath.

Then, silence.

At first, my mind buzzes through its normal loop and goes through all the ways I'm on the precipice of losing everything.

Patty's going to wake up, realize you're a worthless piece of shit, and leave you.

The band will meet another bassist, decide they like them better, and kick you out of the group.

You're going to lose your job and start selling drugs again.

You're pathetic, Tom Hargrove. You always have been. You always will be. Your parents were always right about you.

It only stops when I remember what Cindy once taught me a long time ago. Go back to the breath. The moment. After all, it's the only thing that's guaranteed.

And then, I imagine myself in a grassy plain. It's night. Above, the night sky glitters with millions of stars, the kind of ones I can only dream about.

I see a boy sitting on a blanket in front of me, balancing a guitar in his lap. He's a lot like me. We have the same wavy dark hair and same look in our eyes. He's lost in thought as he strums. After a moment, he stops and sees me. His gaze is sad, longing. He's not just looking at me, he's looking *to* me. He's playing "Two Brothers." The song from the Lincoln show at Disneyland. I don't know why it's in my head. I was a kid when Mom and Dad took Rick and I to Disney. I realize it's the first time I've been back to California since that trip.

My image of the boy is fading, and I have to fight to hold on to him. And I do. But, a moment later, the gong brings us back to the room.

. . .

By the time we walk back to the car, the rain's stopped and I feel more at peace than I have in months. I can tell the others feel similarly.

We don't speak much on the drive back. Before she drops us off, Mila says, "Let me know how it goes. Either way, my brother would love to have you at the Ivy Room."

"Thank you, Mila," Donna says as we all get out.

It's not quite ten, so we go into Frank and Donna's room and play through the song. Once, twice, three times. It's good, what we've come up with, considering the circumstances. Maybe even great.

By eleven, we decide to go to bed and get a good night's sleep.

In our room, I'm about to crawl under the covers when the phone rings. *Who the heck is calling so late?* I give Wally a look. I wonder if it's the front desk wanting to yell at us for something else we did wrong.

"Hello?"

"Oh, thank God, it's you," Patty says. Her speech is slow and slurred.

"Patty-cake, what's wrong?" I say, sitting up.

"I just wanted to hear your voice," she says. "I miss you so much."

"What time is it there?" I ask, now very concerned.

She giggles. "Two in the morning. I have to leave for work in three hours!" She giggles again.

Please tell me she didn't get into our stash and overdo it. Not now. "Is everything okay?"

"It would be better if you were here," she says. "I took the Quaaludes. I'm sorry."

"Honey, how much did you take?"

"I'm fine, *relax*," Patty says.

"How much did you take?" I repeat.

"All of it that was left," Patty says.

Jesus fucking Christ.

"I want you inside me," she says longingly.

"I don't think that's really possible right now." My heart's pounding out of my chest. I wish I could just call Diane and Gracie, but I know it's going to have to be Rick and Jenny since they're so much closer. It's going to come back to bite me, but whatever. I'll deal with the blowback. "Patty-cake, I'm going to call Rick so he can come sit with you, okay?"

"Why? I don't want to talk to Rick!"

"You're going to have to if you ever want me to be inside you again, okay?"

"Ugh... okay," she says with a groan.

"Drink some water in the meantime," I say. "I love you."

"Love you."

I hang up the phone and give Wally a stare. "Patty needs help," I explain.

"Shit," he whispers.

"She'll be fine. She has to be." It's not Patty's fault, but figures this would happen the one time I was about to get a good night's sleep. I take a deep breath in as I dial Rick's number.

Jenny answers. "Hello?"

"Hey, sorry. It's Tom," I explain. "I am so so sorry. Let me talk to Rick. It's an emergency."

"Oh, sure..." she says. I hear them whisper to each other before my brother picks up the phone. His voice is groggy, but I hear his worry. "Tom, what's going on?"

"Can you please go to my house and sit with Patty and

make sure she's okay? She took a bunch of Quaaludes. Take her to the hospital if she needs to, please. But I don't want her to be alone."

Rick groans.

"Come on. This might be life or death."

"It's alright, I can go if you want to sleep," I hear Jenny say in the background.

"No, it's fine," he whispers to her. "I'll go." He speaks back into the phone. "Between you and her, what's our tally right now? I think I'm at nine or ten?"

"Let's save the moral grandstanding for later, okay?" I say impatiently.

"Got it. I am putting on my shoes right now."

"By the way, we have our audition tomorrow morning, so I'll call you once we're back at the hotel."

"Okay. Good luck." He hangs up the phone before I can say more.

I sigh and collapse onto the bed.

Jesus.

Fucking.

Christ.

There goes my night of sleep.

"Rick's going over now," I tell Wally.

"Oh, good," he says. "Hey, mind if we turn the lights off? I'm going to get some shut-eye, if that's okay."

"Go for it," I tell him.

As I stare up at the ceiling, Wally quickly passes out and starts snoring. At about 12:15, I call the house, answering in my lowest whisper.

"Hello?" Rick says.

"Hey. Is she okay?"

"She's fine," he says. "She's drinking water and I'm making her some buttered crackers. She's going to call out of work, but I'll ask Jenny to bring her lunch or something."

"Thank you," I say.

"Yep. Go to bed. I've got it handled."

"Okay. Thanks."

ten

THROUGHOUT THE ENDLESS NIGHT, my mind keeps circling through thoughts of Patty, the audition, and how we might be doing all of this for nothing. Rick said that Patty was going to be fine, but what if she's not? While I'm busy blowing money that was supposed to last for the long haul for a shot in the dark, the love of my life is all alone in that house and suffering. It's true that Patty and I have both had a lot of close calls, but we just have to pace ourselves and everything will be fine.

At some time in the night—or early morning, however you want to frame it—I think of the Dead and Englishtown right before we left. It seems like the crowds have only gotten bigger and are only going to keep moving in that direction. Everyone we met—the guys we walked over to the raceway with, Wally's old classmate, even the girl who was already strung out—we were all there to listen to the same music. The Dead used to live all together in a cramped house just like us. The last few years, I've staked everything on this dream.

Jack's passion for this stuff was infectious. It wasn't six

months from that night I'd listened to the Dead for the first time to when he got his summons. He'd been such a prick about it at first, saying he was going to end the war through music and song alone. "Besides," he'd told me. "I have no plans to die over there. You and I have too much left to do, my friend."

They'd been on the move one day when he'd been shot in the head by someone hiding in the jungle. He hadn't seen it coming. It was instant. He didn't even feel any pain, or so they said.

Hey, you prick, I think. *Guess what? I'm in LA about to have this big audition and I guess I have you to thank for it. So... yeah. Wish you didn't die because the Dead's as awesome as they've ever been and I'm sorry for the way we left things. Wish us luck.*

I don't believe in the afterlife or even in God, but maybe there's a chance Jack heard.

I must have drifted off at some point in the night, because Wally stirs me awake at just before eight. I make a beeline for the phone and try calling Patty. She doesn't answer. Hopefully she's just sleeping, but it's not exactly great for quelling my nerves.

"You ready for this?" Wally asks.

"As I'll ever be," I mutter, rubbing my eyes.

Frank and Donna meet us in the lobby with donuts, but all I can manage to stomach is a few sips of the stale, burnt coffee from the hotel's machine.

On the cab ride over, for the first time, I wonder how many people are up for the gig. Are these other bands just like us? I guess it doesn't matter. I haven't said anything to Donna and Frank about last night and I don't plan to until afterwards so we're not distracted.

. . .

WE HAVE to go up to the very top of a hill to get to Skylark Records. The modernist building is eye catching, and its logo —blue cursive fashioned to look like a bird's wings—looms over the hill.

I eye all the nice cars in the parking lot and even see an Oldsmobile Cutlass. This one's white but good lord, it's still the most beautiful car I've ever seen in my entire life.

We round a circular driveway, and the cab driver lets us off right at the front door. After we pay, the driver wishes us well and we take a minute to gather our things. Then, we take this place in.

Donna's admiring the rainbow of plants in the landscaped courtyard, but I'm looking at the white marble double door— quite possibly, the door to our future.

Once we're all set, we take deep breaths. I wrap my hand against one of the door's angular gold handles and do the honors.

We're met with the trickle of a wall fountain as we go in. As far as lobbies go, it's nice—off-white floors, encased records, and framed news articles decorating the matching walls, and a large, leafy, potted plant in one corner.

The receptionist, a young woman with sandy-blonde hair and an intense stare, is on the phone. We have to awkwardly check in as she keeps taking turns between asking us questions and talking to whoever she's talking to. Finally, she tells us to have a seat because someone will be right with us.

"Be cool, be cool," Frank says to himself once we sink into the cushioned chairs.

A minute or so later, we hear the clicking of high-heeled shoes before Kathy York enters the lobby. "The Hermits?"

We nod. She approaches Donna first, shaking her hand and introducing herself. She isn't very tall, but something about her is imposing. Her bright-orange suit, perfectly manicured black nails, and dark hair pulled back with a clip shows this woman knows who she is and the power she holds.

Frank and I are sitting on opposite sides of Donna, but Kathy turns to me. "Frank?"

"No," I say, awkwardly pointing to him on the other side.

"Oh," Kathy says. "You're not the lead?"

"No," I say, pointing to Frank again. This isn't the first time we've gotten mixed up like this. Is it so unbelievable that a Filipino could not only be the frontman of a band, but married to Donna? Whatever. I try to shrug it off.

Frank's mouth is tight as he waves and shakes her hand. "Thank you for having us, Kathy," he says warmly. "It's really appreciated."

"You're all from Newark, right?" she asks.

We give her a collective nod.

"That's a long ways away," she remarks with a laugh.

You did invite us, Kathy.

A pause as we exchange a nervous look.

"We were in the neighborhood," Frank says after a moment.

She smiles and leads us to the doorway where Rupert Morris greets us.

"Rupert will take it from here," Kathy says, retreating down the hallway shortly thereafter. "Well, you guys are our first group of the day, so enjoy."

Great. There's got to be a lot of people trying out for this.

As Kathy leaves, Rupert looks to me, smiles and shakes my hand. "Hargrove! Good to see you."

"Thank you, sir," I mutter.

"This is going to be recorded?" Donna asks meekly.

"Yes, it's for the Malone's executives to listen to," Rupert says with a smile.

He opens the door. I take a deep breath and gather my courage.

This is actually happening. I'm admiring the ornately carpeted booth and high-tech equipment when I look and see who's right there. Denise is sitting in a swivel chair nearest the glass. She's wearing a fur coat twice the size of her body, one that's way too warm for the studio setting, as she twists her body back and forth. Then, she sees me. We don't have a chance to exchange words before we're being ushered inside the studio itself.

Once we're inside and unpacking our stuff, Rupert joins her, placing his hand on her shoulder. She stands up so he can sit. I watch them watching us for what seems like an eternity as we get ready. I notice their age difference in a way I somehow didn't when I was feet in front of them. He's old enough to be her dad.

I don't know that this is the man I ever would have pictured Denise with.

My thought is interrupted by Rupert's voice coming over the loudspeaker.

"Alright, Hermits. Do you have something for us?"

"We do," Frank manages.

"Whenever you're ready."

We have to start over not once, not twice, but three times because Frank keeps messing up the vocals. After the second time, Rupert says, "Relax. All of you. I can tell you're nervous, okay?"

I think of us from the day before and Donna holding up the dress. And I picture our song playing over a loudspeaker.

We get a take that we feel pretty good about.

After they thank us for our time, it's hard to process the fact that this is it and that it's out of our hands now.

Back in the booth, Denise stands up as we walk out.

"When will decisions be made?" Donna asks Rupert.

"Well, that's up to Malone's, but I know that they want to move forward by November. So, hang tight," Rupert says.

Donna and Rupert continue to chat as I process this. Denise and I lock eyes.

"Hi," she whispers.

"Hi," I say. "What are you doing here?"

"I wanted to watch," she says. "Spend some time with my husband, too. Is that a crime?"

"No."

"Why'd you disappear the other day?" she asks.

I open my mouth, trying to think of what to say. I'm really not in the mood for this. Still, I don't have a chance to speak because Rupert has just turned to us. He puts his arm around Denise and brings her in close. "Denny tells me you guys are going to be at the Ivy Room," Rupert says.

"Oh, well..." I look back at Frank, Wally, and Donna. "I don't think that's set in stone yet."

Denise gives me a pleading look.

"It's another month, at least?" I ask Rupert. "Before we hear?"

"I'm not Malone's, so I can't say for sure," he says. "But we'll be in touch."

As we exit out to the lobby, we see two other bands. One's a duo—a guy and a girl—and the other group is a group of four. They're taking up all the seats so we have to stand. The receptionist is on the phone again, so, I have to wait what seems like an agonizing amount of time before I ask if it's free.

"Oh, well you can't use this one, but there's a payphone for guests outside," she says.

Oh, whatever.

"I got it, guys," I tell my bandmates, just as Kathy's entered to call the duo forward.

Once outside, I do at least two circles of the place before I find it tucked away into a hidden corner. I get all the way over before I realize I my wallet's back in the lobby.

I'd sooner walk all the way down the hill if we didn't have our equipment.

When I go back in, Frank and Donna are sitting and Wally's chatting animatedly with the receptionist.

I snag my wallet, dart back out to the booth, and call.

They tell me they'll be there in fifteen minutes.

WALLY'S still talking to the receptionist as I walk in. I find an empty space on the wall, lean back, and let out a breath. My body's still so tight from the stress and I'm basically running on fumes, but it's not a minute before the receptionist gets my attention.

"Sir, please don't lean on that, thank you," she says.

I take a step away, not able to help my irritated inhale.

"It's just, it could damage the displays," she says. She and Wally pick up their conversation right where they left off.

I look at the group of four, all of them young guys. Each

one has a slightly different shade of brown, clean-cut hair, so when they all sit in a certain order, I feel like I'm looking at a color gradient.

"None of us have dyed our hair, in case you're wondering," the one with the darkest hair says.

"Cool," I manage. I notice their outfits for the first time—they're dressed like members of a barbershop quartet. Of course they're a fucking barbershop quartet. I didn't see the duo carrying any instruments either. Two singing groups. Us. I guess it depends on what they're looking for.

Finally, our cab pulls up.

"You're going to tell us about your girlfriend?" I ask Wally once we get in the car and on the road.

"Oh, Audrey?" Wally asks. "We're both from Doylestown, so just trading stories."

"She was pretty cute," Donna teases.

"I don't know, she kind of seems like she had a stick up her ass," I say.

"Tom!" Donna exclaims.

I open my mouth to speak, but Wally waves me off.

"It's fine," he says. "Besides, I'm never going to see her again."

"You will if we get this gig," Donna teases.

Wally doesn't respond to this, but his cheeks turn red.

It's a few minutes of ensuing silence on the road before Donna says, "I think we should take Ivy's, though. I don't know about you guys, I'm feeling good, but we should still explore our options."

"I do too," Frank agrees.

"So do I," Wally says.

Everyone looks to me. "Yeah, of course—"

"But?" Donna says.

"Patty called me strung out last night and could have overdosed," I say. "I just want to call her before we decide anything."

"Oh my God. Is she okay?" Donna asks.

"Yeah, Rick came over and helped her. She'll be fine," I say. "But still."

"Well, if we do Ivy's, maybe she could come here," Donna offers. "Even for a visit."

"We'll see," I say. "Anyway, what about work? For us?"

"The store doesn't care if I'm gone," Donna says. "If they do, so what? Besides, I'm sure there's print shops out here that could use an extra pair of hands when we're not performing."

"Same," Wally says. "I mean, I don't really care if I get fired. It's not really ice cream season anymore anyway."

"I'll tell the office there was an emergency with my grandparents and I'll be in the Philippines and completely unreachable," Frank says mischievously.

"You're cruel," I manage.

"I've got like two weeks of vacation, anyway. I'll figure the rest out," he says.

They all look at me as I stare blankly out the window.

"What?" Donna says to me.

"You know what," I whisper.

"Oh!" she exclaims, laying on the drama. "Whatever will Archie and Edith Bunker do without their darling son to keep track of hardware sales? However will the world go on turning?"

"Please don't call them that," I say. Donna finds the comparison a little too funny and it's not what I need to be thinking about. "Just please don't, okay? Not right now."

"You're three against one," Frank says after a moment. "Nothing's stopping you from going back."

"What the fuck? When did I ever say I wanted to go back? I'm concerned about work and about Patty—"

"Bring her out here."

"We just need to make sure we're not putting all of our eggs in one basket. What if it doesn't work out?"

"What if it does?" Donna says plainly.

"So, it's all set?" I ask. "The gig?"

"We just have to say the word," Donna says. "I've got Mila Potter's number."

"Let me call Patty when we get back to the hotel, okay?" I say. "And see what she thinks."

BACK IN THE HOTEL ROOM, I cross my fingers that she's going to answer.

I'm in luck.

"Tom, oh my gosh," she says. "I'm so sorry."

"Don't mention it."

"I'm fine... Jenny came by with lunch and last night... everything's really hard. I just wanted it to stop."

"I understand. I wish I was there to help."

"You don't have to worry about me. Between working and Diane, I'm so busy. My schedule's changing every day, otherwise I'd let you know, but—"

"I'm just happy you're okay, Patty-cake." Eventually, I spit out everything I have to tell her. Not just about how the Malone's audition went, but this offer that we suddenly have to stay in LA and perform, especially considering what happened last night.

She's silent for a while.

"Well, say something," I finally say.

"I mean, it's amazing. I think you guys should do it," Patty remarks.

"You're probably too busy to come out here, huh?" I say.

"I mean, I'd love to," she replies. "I'll have to see if I can get the time off and make sure Diane will be okay. I'll let you know."

"I miss you," I tell her.

"Me too."

"I wish I could hold you in my arms."

"We'll see each other again soon," she promises.

"Are you sure you're going to be okay?"

"Yeah," she says. "Of course. Tripping alone's no fun anyway."

"Do you want to guess how we got this gig?" I ask her.

"How?"

"We met Mila Potter at Denise's party and it's her brother that owns this club."

I can picture Patty's smile. "Wow."

"Yeah, she took us meditating last night," I explain.

"What's she like? What's Denise like?"

"Mila's elegant and refined and Denise is very sweet."

"Cool," she says.

I smile. "I'm gonna go. I love you."

"I love you too."

After we hang up, I go next door. Wally trails behind me as I give Donna the go-ahead to call Mila.

We all watch as they talk for a few minutes, and we make plans to come in the next day for an audition as a formality.

After she hangs up, Donna announces to us, "Apparently, as long as we don't completely suck, it's going to be fine."

We can only hope.

"What about a place to live?" I ask.

"We'll find a rental or something," she says.

"That'll be expensive," I reply.

"What's some temporary suffering for a chance that everything's going to start going our way?"

THE NEXT DAY, we take a cab ride over to the Ivy Room.

In Newark, we've played at a lot of places just like it. This is a step or two above them, with floors carpeted blue and its seats a matching shade of leather. The wood-paneled walls are much the same. Black-and-white pictures of various LA landscapes decorate them, secured behind thick frames.

Mila's brother, Rob, doesn't have much to say. We hadn't discussed what to play or what he even wanted us to play, so we default to our standard: Donovan's "Wear Your Love Like Heaven."

"Only covers?" Rob says once we're finished. "Don't you guys write?"

Frank shrugs. "People like our version, and I don't know if we're the best writers in the world."

"I didn't say it was a bad thing." Rob laughs, and I notice he's at looking Donna up and down.

Is he leering at her?

"I think you guys should play whatever you want to play," Rob says. He leans forward. He shakes Donna's hand first. "Welcome to the Ivy Room, Hermits." It seems to linger before he moves onto the rest of us. I see the wedding ring on his finger. Maybe I'm reading too much into things or searching for a reason why this isn't going to work out.

Just like that, we sign contracts to perform twice a week for at least the next month. Depending on how things go, they'll consider extending it.

In the cab, I still feel uneasy, and I need to know that I'm just imagining things. "What do we all think of Rob Potter?"

"He seems nice," Donna says nonchalantly. "Why do you ask?"

"Never mind," I say. "Just curious."

It's my imagination for sure.

THE HOUSE down the street we want—the only place in walking distance to the Ivy Room with space for all of us—is $600 a month, putting us at $750 when we include the extra week. I only have about $300 left, and the others remind me we're going to need to figure out flights back, so we split the cost four ways. The place itself is smack in the middle of a steep hill. It's not Laurel Canyon, but away from the road, down a tree-lined cobblestone path, it might as well be. It's enough to distract me from the fact that all I have to my name is $100 plus my last $180 paycheck from Mom and Dad.

After we've settled into the house, I call my dad as my bandmates watch me.

"Thomas," he says. "How are things going?"

"They're good. Hey, we just got a gig so we're going to be out here for the next month," I say. "So I won't be at work."

"What do you mean? When are you going to be back?"

"I don't know," I tell him. "At least a month. Maybe more."

"You can't be gone for a month," Dad says. "What do you expect us to do?"

"I don't know," I say dryly. "Figure it out?"

"You can have a week, but then I expect you back here," he says.

"I can't be back in a week," I tell him. "We just signed a contract for the next month."

"If you're quitting, you need to say so. Because we'd need to hire someone else."

"Then I quit," I say, hanging up the phone before he can say more.

They all smile and clap, and I feel more satisfied that I have in a long time.

Still, I feel the knots clenching up in my stomach.

We're all in now.

eleven

JUST AS THINGS are starting to get cold and frosty back home, I'm sitting with my bandmates on the lawn of our rented house. We're sharing a joint, relaxing for the afternoon while we get ready for our first day at the gig.

Since we've settled in, Wally finishes Michael Rooney's book and gives it to me to borrow. I'm only a few chapters in, so I'm still at the early years, right as he started to realize that acting was a worthwhile escape from his tumultuous home life and poverty. It's hard to wrap my head around how much I relate to him. If he can start from nothing and make something of himself, then why can't I? I know Denise had humble upbringings herself. What makes them different from us?

It's Tuesday, so they don't expect a big crowd, which is perfect for us to get our feet wet. It's so nice performing, even if it's to about ten people, that I forget about Malone's and everything else that's at stake.

We're packing up in the green room afterwards when Rob

comes to check in. "Great show tonight," he says. "You have talent."

"Thank you," Donna manages.

"You're quite welcome," Rob says. "See you Friday."

He leaves, and all of us look at each other.

"Hear that?" Frank says. "We have talent."

"Our breakthrough is just around the corner. I can feel it," I say sarcastically.

Frank and Wally both snicker, but Donna is quiet. Distant.

"Sweetheart, what's wrong?" Frank asks her.

"No one was there," she mutters, fighting tears.

"I counted at least one or two," Frank says with a wry smile.

Donna descends into tears now as Frank comforts her. "What's the point of trying?"

"I know I do because I like music and I like you, and I also like those two things together," Frank tells her.

"It beats sitting on my ass and giving my life to Baskin-Robbins, that's for sure," Wally says. "I think I'd die or drive myself crazy if we didn't have this."

"I'm with Wally and Frank" is all I say.

Donna's still crying. "It's never enough. It's never going to be enough."

"Enough for what, sweetie?" Frank asks.

"Getting to breathe," she says. "Getting to live past tomorrow. When do we get to stop busting our asses for fucking breadcrumbs and just live?"

"Hey," Frank tells her. "We've had one show. Let's not jump to conclusions."

He smiles at her, kisses her, and then we start packing up our things.

Over the next few days, we try to find more work. But that ends up being harder than we thought. Donna can't find anywhere that's hiring on a temporary basis. Wally finds a restaurant that's interested in him but the hours they want conflict with what we've already got to perform at the Ivy. As for me, nothing's around that even matches my skills.

By Friday, we're no closer to figuring it out. There's more people, but it still goes by uneventfully. After, Wally, Frank, and I pack up in the green room and are all painfully aware of Rob and Donna talking in the hallway. We can't quite hear what they're saying.

After a beat or two, Donna enters, looking tired. Rob passes by and glares at all of us but says nothing.

"What was that about?" I ask her.

"Rob wanted to take me out for a drink," Donna says. "Just me."

Frank raises his eyebrow.

"He said it was to talk about our image, maybe go over like record labels where we could be a good fit? I don't know. I said, 'we all have to be there, or at least my husband does.' And he was like, 'no, forget about it.'" She sighs.

"If he touches you—" Frank starts.

"I don't think it was like *that*," she says. "Forget I brought it up."

"I will *not* forget that you brought it up!" Frank exclaims

"He's not a creep. I think I'm overreacting," Donna says. "Please, drop it. I don't want to jeopardize the gig."

Frank gives up after this.

. . .

WE'VE JUST GOTTEN BACK to the house when the phone rings. I'm the closest to it, so I answer.

"Tom? Is that you?" It's Denise. Her speech is slurred. She sounds depressed.

"Denise?" I confirm.

"Hi... I got your number for Mila, who got it from Rob. Um... if you're not busy, can you come to my house?"

I pause, aware of everyone else's eyes on me.

"I'm having a party. I forgot to invite you, but I'm inviting you now. Bring your bandmates, too!"

"Let me ask," I say. I'm not really sure I want to go, but her tone of voice is worrying. I guess I'll tag along if anyone else is interested.

I'm about to turn around to face them when she says, "Tom, I have to go."

"Wait, let me..." I start.

She hangs up before I can say more.

Frank, Donna, Wally, and I exchange looks.

"Anyone want to go to a party at Denise's?" I ask.

None of them have time to reply before the phone rings again.

"Denise?" I say.

"Who's Denise?" Diane's voice calls.

Shit. "Sorry, it's Tom."

"Hello, Tom, nice to meet you, my name is Diane," she replies sarcastically. "I don't think we've been introduced."

I rush out the first half-baked lie that comes to my head. "Sorry, Denise is the landlady that we're renting this house from." She doesn't respond, so I add, "How are you?"

"Um, I'm okay. Is this a good time to talk?"

My heart pounds. Uh-oh. What happened now? I shoo the

others away and grip the receiver tight in my hands. "Yeah. You sound good, by the way."

"I'm fine," she says dismissively. "Hey. I'm worried about Patty. There was a little situation at work today. She was caught stealing some pain medication that was meant for her patients and using it for herself. She is very, very, *very* lucky that her boss let her off with a stern warning. But that only happened after I begged for him not to fire her. But if it happens again, she has no recourse."

I don't know what to say. "Thanks for telling me."

"I feel responsible," Diane says. "I know I wasn't always the best influence on her after our mom and dad, but she keeps the habit under control when you're around."

"Patty's a grown adult. She can take care of herself," I say.

"Right now, she can't." Diane sighs. "I kept telling her to come out there and visit you. The back and forth between her and Gracie is driving me crazy. Being a pity case is worse than the fucking disease." When I don't say anything, she adds, more inaudibly, "Part of me wishes I would just croak already."

"Diane, don't talk like that," I say.

"I'm sorry," she says with a scoff. "Too much, too soon?'"

"Just a bit."

"Anyways, Tom," she continues. "My point is, I think she needs to get back on her feet before she can think about taking any kind of trip."

"What do you want me to do?" I say after a while. Of course she can't come out to LA. I figured in the back of my mind that it wasn't going to work out, but I think I let myself hope that it would.

Man, I really miss her.

"Well," Diane says, "she's going to stay with us for at least a couple of days, and Gracie will go back to Newark with her to check on the house. I would if I could, but I don't want to push it."

"Okay" is all I'm able to muster.

"Just keep us posted on when you end up coming back," she says.

"Sure, I will."

"Have a good night," Diane says, hanging up the phone.

I stand there for a moment, rubbing my eyes as I process what I've just heard.

I'm very glad that Patty didn't lose her job, but I can't help but feel guilty that I'm not there. At least she has Diane and Gracie.

I'll call her tomorrow and figure out what's going on. I realize that Donna's migrated back into the living room. She and I lock eyes.

"I don't think anyone wants to go to Denise's, but if you do, feel free," she says. "Who was on the phone earlier?"

"Diane," I tell her.

I realize I can't move. My body feels like it's just become a ten ton weight.

Diane's going to die. I can't picture the world without her. It shouldn't be her time, and it's not fair that it is.

One day, I'll be dead too.

So will Frank, Wally, Donna, Patty, Gracie, Denise, Rick, Jenny, my parents, Rupert Morris, Kathy York...

As will the girl at the hotel's front desk, Audrey the Skylark receptionist, and the kid that yelled at us about the noise complaints.

So will everyone.

All of this—the music, the parties, working forty hours a week—it's all just a distraction from the inevitable.

I don't think any of that ever hit me, at least not fully, until just now.

I start to cry.

"Tom..." Donna starts. "Please. I've done enough of that for all of us lately."

"I think I just realized that I'm going to die one day," I tell her half jokingly.

"Well, to quote a famous poet," Donna says. "No one here gets out alive."

"Put that on my gravestone," I tell her with a smile. "I'm serious." I really am. That would be the coolest epitaph ever.

THE NEXT MORNING, I call Diane back. She passes me to Patty.

"What were you thinking?" I ask her. "Stealing from your job?"

"I wasn't. I just... I didn't want to make you mad by taking more of the stash, and I just wanted to not feel anything for a little while," she says. "I'm so ashamed of myself."

"Well, it's looking like we'll be back soon," I tell her. I have no idea why I just said that. But call it a gut feeling based on the way things have been going so far.

"Really?" Patty says.

"Really."

THE NEXT TWO weeks come and go. In the meantime, when we're not performing, there's not much to do except sit around with my own thoughts. During the day, I end up taking long walks in the neighborhood. On one of them, it hits me that $37.50 a week, after our fee's split four ways, still evens out to about what I make at the store. And that's working six hours a week.

Maybe we're not as lost as my parents and people like them think we are.

Patty ends up going back to the house at the start of our third week and insists to me over and over that she's fine. I feel guilty that things are so hard for her. If I was back in Newark or she was out there, maybe things would be different.

As we head into week four, our money's running dry. It's a nice night, so we're all sitting outside with beer when Donna says, "I wonder what's going on with Malone's. It'd be nice to know."

That night, we don't get news about Malone's, but we do have a special guest. I notice her sitting near the back. She's dressed casually in jeans and a turtleneck sweater and sunglasses over her eyes, but I recognize Denise immediately.

I take a deep breath as we continue our set.

She catches me right as we start to pack up, and Rob approaches Donna, asking if she could talk. I watch out of the corner of my eye as they disappear in one direction, and Denise pulls me in another.

"Hi," she says.

"Hi. I was going to call you back the other night, but I didn't have your number—"

"It's okay." She makes sure no one else is around before she takes her sunglasses off. I see it right away. The bruise over her eye.

"What happened to you?" I ask.

"I egged Rupert on," she says.

"Denise..."

She pulls the collar of her turtleneck down and I see there's another bruise there too.

Words fail me.

"He has a temper," she explains. "It doesn't take much to set it off. He thinks..."

I stare.

"You know what. Never mind. It doesn't matter."

"Okay," I manage, as empathetically as I possibly can. "What do you want me to do?"

"Nothing," she says. "I just came to see you play. I haven't had a chance to do that yet. Anyway, it was really nice. Um... how long are you staying in town for?"

"I don't know," I say. "We might go back after next week."

Her face falls. "Aww. Why?"

"Well, unless something magically happens with Malone's or this contract gets extended, it doesn't seem like it's working out too well. Besides, we're almost out of money."

Denise sighs. "Okay. I can maybe talk to Kathy and see what's going on."

"If it's not too much trouble," I tell her.

She shakes her head.

"When's your next show?"

"Friday."

After a moment, she takes a pen out of her jean pocket and writes an address on my hand. "Meet me here after that. Around midnight."

"Where is this?" I ask.

"Just go to the address. Find an excuse to split off and we'll talk, okay? I promise I'll have an answer from Kathy by then."

I don't have a chance to respond. I've barely looked at the address before she's gone, like she was never there at all.

I see Frank, Donna, and Wally talking, their expressions grim. After a moment, I pull my shirt sleeve down to hide the address and join their circle.

"Rob really appreciates everything we've done this past month but he will not be needing us going forward. We'll be done after Friday," Donna says dryly, automatically. She wipes a tear from her eye.

"What did Denise Peck want?" Frank asks casually.

"She was just saying hi," I remark.

"Mm-hmm."

I'm not in the mood to fight him on this, so I don't say anything.

"Rob Potter's going to have a piece of my mind, that's for sure," Frank tells Donna. "Fuck that guy. And fuck him for wasting our time."

"Frank, please. Please don't mess this up. I'd like to get paid."

"Did they say why they won't be keeping us on?" I ask.

Donna shrugs. "We weren't good enough, I guess."

On the walk home, we all have to take a moment to process.

"I guess we have no choice but to leave," Wally finally says.

"I like LA," Donna whispers. "Twenty-thousand dollars would sure be nice right about now."

"Yeah..." Frank says.

"Well, let's give them one last great show," I say.

"I have a confession to make, you guys," Wally admits. "I called Skylark and invited Audrey to come to one of our gigs."

"Proud of you, man. That took guts," Frank says.

"No," Wally corrects. "She turned me down."

"You want to be away from it?" I ask.

Wally nods. "Yeah, I guess."

"You'll find someone, don't worry," I say. Sometimes I wonder how Wally feels being our fifth wheel. His last girlfriend was around before I knew him and he doesn't ever talk about her.

"Says the guy that gets Denise Peck to show up just because," he says.

"Haha," I say.

We keep walking in silence.

I'm so exhausted with everything.

Our last hope is Malone's magically coming through.

I can only find out when I meet Denise.

twelve

EVERYTHING about our last show just seems to mock us. All the people who've never had to struggle for money a day in their life are staring, judging us.

I miss home. Even if I don't know what I'm going to do for work when I get back—although I'm pretty sure I can convince Dad to hire me back—home has Patty.

I've been avoiding calling her because I don't want her to catch on to how depressed I really am, and how worthless I feel, especially as I face down the barrel of the realization that I've zapped all of my savings for absolutely nothing.

I feel bad for Wally too, because even though he acts cool and easy-going all the time I can tell he's disappointed about Audrey.

Still, by the time the show nears its end, I'm hopeful that this is going to be the moment where everything turns around. This is how it usually works out with these sorts of stories, right?

The night before, Denise's number was starting to fade

from my hand, so I wrote it down and kept the slip of paper secure in my pocket.

We're packing up and we all notice Rob walking down the hallway. Wally, Donna and I avert his gaze, but Frank stands up and punches Rob in the face.

Donna screams.

"Stay away from my wife!" Frank yells.

It takes Wally and I both to tear Frank off him.

Blood drips from Rob's nose. "You four better get out of here right now or things are about to get ugly."

We do.

"WHAT THE FUCK is wrong with you?" Donna says to Frank as we all walk back.

"What the fuck is wrong with *me*?!" he retorts.

"Whoa, whoa, whoa. What's going on?" I cut in.

"You want to tell them what happened, Donna?" Frank yells.

"Lower your voice!" Donna says. "We're in public! And I was handling it!"

"As your husband, it's my job to protect you from men like that!"

"I don't need your protection!" Donna yells. "I told him no. I wanted to get our check, get out of there, and never see him again! And now, not only have we been stiffed, but you could have gotten arrested!"

"Wait, so what exactly happened?" Wally asks.

"Rob Potter is a scumbag. That's all you need to know," Frank says.

I don't think we're going to get a straight answer any time soon. But I know that I need to get away.

By the time we get back and settled, it's already time to go.

Wally, Frank, and Donna are all sitting quietly on the couch as I start to walk out.

"Where are you going?" Frank asks.

"For a walk," I say.

"Now?"

"Yes, now," I repeat.

"Alright, well, when you're back we need to talk about our plan. Because we've got like three days left on this place and just enough for flights back."

"Sounds about right," I say without looking back at them.

I HITCH a ride and about forty minutes later, I'm on the Sunset Strip. I almost turn back when I see where Denise has led me. Of course it's here.

The Lantern Club. It looks abandoned. Its cursive, turquoise sign above an empty marquee has seen better days. Even though all the lights are off, I can just make out the musty red carpet that probably was the height of elegance once.

I try the door. At first, I think it's locked. I convince myself this was all some sort of misunderstanding, but when I push a little harder, it opens. I'm met with the smell of musty wood and velvet.

It's not a big space. Between not knowing where the light switch is and not wanting to draw attention to myself, I'm forced to rely on the moonlight to make out details. I look back at the door. Back in the day, Jack and I would have lived for something like this. And now, all I can think of is wanting to go back to the house.

I don't know when the last time someone was inside here was, but it feels like it's been years. You'd never be able to get away with making a building this gaudy today. It must have already been in disrepair by the time Denise first walked through these doors. The wood accents and other modernist updates to the ticket booth and the concession stand clash with the original design and reek of desperation.

Then, I see her picture on the poster. She's posing with a guitar, wearing lavender, her hair teased. "DENISE PECK, THE GIRL WONDER. EVERY WEDNESDAY AND FRIDAY NIGHT," it says in block white lettering, beside the date of the first show. "AUGUST 5TH, 1970." She's beaming. There's her pretty, crooked smile again. I wish she would make a point to show it off.

That's when I hear the sound of an acoustic guitar coming from the theater. And her voice. It's "Smile." The Nat King Cole song. Without any backing tracks or recording equipment, I didn't know her voice could sound like this.

I make my way into the theater. The lights are on. It's small. Maybe a hundred seats at most. She's smack in the center of the audience, dressed in a simple jeans and blouse. No makeup, no furs. Just a twenty-one-year-old girl. Donna really is her doppelgänger. Or maybe it's the other way around. I remind myself that Denise is younger than her, than all of us.

I sit behind her, and I let her finish the song. If there's any unspoken rules in life, it's that you never interrupt Denise Peck. Once she does, she puts her guitar aside and gestures for me to sit next to her.

I do.

"I wasn't sure if you'd come," she tells me.

"Hey, is it okay that we're here?" I ask.

Denise shrugs. "I dunno. Who cares? The maintenance guy unlocks it for me when I ask. He'll lock after we leave." As she slurs her words, I smell bourbon on her breath. I know I can't judge, as a stiff drink doesn't sound half bad myself.

"Where is he now?"

"Who knows?" she says. "I gave him some money. He said he went to get food but he's probably screwing some whore for all I know."

"Why are we here, Denise?" I ask.

She looks back at the stage. As she does, I see the bruises from the other night on her neck and eye. "This is where Rupert sat when he came to my first show here." Then, to me. "Do you know how old I was?"

I shake my head.

"Fourteen."

"And how old do you think I was the first time we had sex?"

"I don't know."

"Seventeen." She sniffles. "He told me he'd been trying to control himself since the day we met because I was just that beautiful and he couldn't wait anymore." She wipes away a tear. "What's a girl to do when someone handsome and charming and kind tells you that he can't live without you?"

I just look at her.

"I thought I'd found my Prince Charming and this was going to be my happily ever after," Denise says. "I don't know when it changed or why or what I did to get here."

I look at the bruises again. They're black and blue. "You

could have anyone you want," I say. "I think he knows that, too."

"Why could I have anyone I want?" she asks with a scoff.

I stare at her. "Because."

"What's your girlfriend's name again?" I can really hear her slurred speech now.

"Patty."

"Patty. That's right," Denise repeats. "Why isn't she here with you?"

"Long story," I say.

"Are you two fighting?"

"No, it's not that."

"So, bring her out here," she says. "Your dream isn't complete without her."

"We're going to go back to Newark," I tell Denise. "We have to."

She leans back in her chair. "All five of you live in a house together, right?"

I nod. While I'm enjoying the chat, I want to get to the reason I'm here. "So, what did Kathy say?"

Denise sighs. "They're going with someone else. She said that there was something missing."

"Oh," I say. "What's missing?"

"She didn't explain. I don't know. I'm not her."

"Sure," I mutter, letting what she just said sink in. We so needed good news. Not this. "Wait, what do you mean, *she* said something's missing?" From the look Denise gives me, it immediately hits. "Malone's never even heard our tape, did they?"

Her face tightens. "I'm sorry," she says. "But... I think you're going to look back and think this was a blessing in disguise."

"All this to tell me it's a no?" I say, angry now.

Denise says nothing. Instead, I see her sniffling again. "Come on. It's just one no."

"Easy for you to say," I reply, not able to hide the resentment in my voice.

"What do you mean?"

"Because our 'one no' means we need to go back because we can't afford to stay here anymore," I explain, irritated. "Some people in this world actually have to think about money, Denise. One night at the Chateau? You book it without a second thought. That was a fourth of my life savings. To get out here, another half? To stay for a month for nothing? It's all gone. Everything I've worked for since my best friend died and my girlfriend cheated on me."

"Patty?" she says.

"No," I snap. "Not her... It's the past, and anyway, it doesn't matter."

Denise stares at me, her eyes glassy. Her breaths are heavy for a moment before she finally speaks, whispering, "You can't let this stop you."

I nod and consider, forcing myself to calm down. We were expecting this, anyways. A moment later, I'm just numb.

"It's going to be okay," Denise says. "I promise."

"Sure," I whisper.

"Anyway, I thought you could stay a while. We could talk. No expectations, for once."

"Okay," I say. Everything in this musty auditorium is blurry and out of focus, like I'm drowning in radio static. But once Denise reaches into my soul with those rich, brown eyes, I'm back in tune.

I can't believe I could barely look her in the eye when we

first met. I think she's more beautiful like this than any perfume ad or album cover could ever convey.

After a moment, she smiles, showing off her crooked teeth again.

As her cheeks turn red, I say, "why do you never let anyone see you smile?"

Denise's face tightens and I see her start to cry. "Maybe people wouldn't like me if they knew I wasn't perfect."

"What if they would like you more?"

"I hate my smile," she says.

"So why not fix it?"

"Because I'm afraid it'll change my voice. Even if it doesn't, it's the last reminder of who I was before." She wipes a tear from her eye and adds, "You know, sometimes... I'm awake at night, all alone, and I'm tempted to take a map, find a place where nobody knows my name and just... go there to start life all over again. Finally learn how to drive."

"You don't know how?" I ask.

Denise shakes her head. "I left home before I could learn. And Rupert always said..."

"What?"

"There's no point because I wouldn't ever need to drive myself around," she says tiredly, managing a smile. "You know what kind of car I'd want? One of those little Volkswagen Bugs. A yellow one. Small and cute and only for me."

Somehow, I'm not surprised she wants a simple car. But I don't know what to make of it.

I watch Denise's face fall as she inhales. "I wish someone would just talk to me like I'm a person for once."

"I will," I whisper.

Some light floods back into her eyes. "Anyway, the five of

you all living together? It takes me back to when I was at this boarding house in Highland Park. I had to take three buses to get here to the Lantern," she says. "But I took the first thing I could get, both with housing and with work. I had to get out of Kansas, away from my parents."

"Yeah?" I say.

"My dad would come into my room sometimes, and my mom definitely knew, but she'd drink so she didn't have to deal with it."

"Deal with what?"

"Don't make me say it," Denise mutters.

I focus in on her face, realizing, and wrap her in a hug. I hope, for her sake, that she doesn't remember this in the morning.

"One day, I told my parents that they could go fuck themselves. I got my guitar, got on a bus, and I never looked back. I didn't learn keys until *The Edge of Eden*, you know." She sniffles. "Anyways, I'm jealous of you guys."

I blink. "What do you mean?"

Her eyes are glued to the stage as she tells me. "I mean I'm jealous, because you four seem really happy together. And I haven't met Patty, because you didn't bring her, but I bet she's just as cute as a button. But it's been a long time since I've been around anyone who is this excited about music. You, your band, for you, it's enough. You get to do it and love it without trying to be everyone's perfect fantasy."

"Well, we don't have a manager or record label or fans but I do know a thing or two about meeting expectations," I say wryly.

"I'm your fan," Denise says. She notices my disbelieving

reaction and adds, "I'm not just saying that. I'm serious. Your music was really nice."

All I can do is whisper a barely audible "thanks."

In response, she hands me her guitar. Holding it, my hands shake. "Play me something."

"Like what?"

"The first song that made you love music," Denise says. "You heard mine earlier."

"Nat King Cole?"

Denise nods. "My first love."

I find myself smiling. "Really?"

"I used to sneak his records to my friend Suzy's house because my parents thought it was improper." Denise laughs. "Nat King Cole, improper? Can you fucking imagine?"

"Why?"

Denise gives me a tired look. "Why do you think?"

I have nothing to say.

"I couldn't stop crying the day he died because I always thought, no matter what, if he could create such beautiful music, then the world can't be such a bad place, right? We can't all be beyond saving?"

As she talks, all I can do is nod along.

"And if he could do it while standing up to bigots, what excuse did I have?" She sniffles.

I purse my lips, blinking back tears myself as I feel her guitar in my hands. It's weathered and worn. "How long have you had this?"

"It's a 1956 original," Denise says. "Anyway, I want to hear your song."

I run my fingers over the strings a few times, thinking. The answer is obvious, even if I pause at tapping into the memory.

I do anyway.

A moment later, I'm singing "Somewhere." My dry voice reminds me of why I'll never be the lead, but Denise seems to be a captive audience, leaning against the chair of the seat and close to me.

When I'm done, she claps and asks, "why that one?"

"When I was a kid, my mom and dad took me and my brother to New York and we saw the original cast of *West Side Story...*"

Suddenly, I'm overwhelmed by the tears that well in my eyes. I was all of five years old and I remember it like it was yesterday. Because it was winter and we'd gone to a matinee, later in the day we went ice skating at Rockefeller Center. I'd fallen, started crying and Mom had taken me to the bathroom to get me bandaged up.

"It's just a scratch, Tommy. But you know what? I heard little boys who fall down are entitled to one free hot chocolate."

I can't stop myself from crying now.

"Hey, it's okay," Denise says, rubbing her hand up and down my arm. "I'm sorry."

I can't bring myself to respond. Thoughts of Diane, of Patty, of the fact that we came here for nothing are spinning. After a moment, I sit up and manage to dry my tears.

"Tom, can I ask you a question?"

"Sure," I mutter, handing her back her guitar, which she limply takes.

"How long do you think you're going to live?"

"Huh?"

She repeats the question.

"I don't know," I say, looking towards the empty stage. "I

guess I never really thought about it. But I'd like to think I'll be old and gray. Someday."

"Sitting in your chair, around a fire, kids, grandkids, a dog..." Denise says.

The thought makes me smile. "Something like that, yeah."

"I'll be surprised if I even make twenty-seven," Denise whispers.

"You could leave Rupert, you know," I say.

Denise sniffles. "Yeah, I could."

I have about a split second to realize what's about to happen before it does, and even less time to react. She'd been inching closer to me this whole time, but I didn't register it until she brought her lips to mine and her hands to my cheeks.

It's automatic, the way I reciprocate. My hands moving to her shoulders. Providing just what she needs from me. Being this wanted without anything else being expected of me.

She kisses me deeper and gets onto my lap.

"This okay?" she whispers. The bourbon on her breath is overwhelming now.

My words don't come. She takes her shirt off. She wasn't wearing a bra under that white blouse, and I have a moment to stare at her breasts and the freckles all over her body. I know I should stop, but I can't. It's like I'm immobile, and there's nothing I can do but go along and let this happen.

She gets closer to me. The bourbon smell somehow gets more potent as she moves her hand to my shirt collar. It comes off, too.

As she runs her fingers across my lips, I can't quell the rush that floods through me.

I look at her freckled body.

Freckles. Patty.

Oh, God.

What the fuck have I done?

She's about to lean into kiss me again when I pull away.

"I'm sorry. I can't—"

"Uh-huh." Denise's face falls as she gets off me, puts her shirt back on, and collapses into her seat. Her face tightens and not a second later she's sobbing.

My body is lead as I put my shirt back on, then just sit and stare.

"Just go, please," she wails.

"Denise," I start.

"Just go. I'm sorry."

thirteen

JACK'S VOICE, calling out to me from 1971, rings through the dark night as I try to hitch a ride.

"*I'm sorry. I'm sorry. I'm sorry.*"

I still felt the tingle of his lips on mine as I forced myself to look up from the couch and at him.

"I'm so stupid," he said. "Just forget this happened, please. It wasn't fair to you, to Cindy. I just..."

"What?" I managed.

We were at his apartment, sitting on his couch. He wanted to see me one last time before he went away. Cindy had already said her goodbyes—she was in Cleveland for a gymnastics meet. He'd been surprisingly jovial for someone who was shipping out to Vietnam in the morning. He'd brushed my hand first as I'd rolled a joint for the two of us. It wasn't the first time we'd touched in a way that was more than just... I don't know what. He'd always shrugged it off as accidental, but I think he wanted it to happen.

"I understand if you want to go," he said after a while.

"I am staying *right* here," I told him.

He sniffled. His eyes were bleary.

I thought of an afternoon in 1968, near the end of sophomore year. I'd come over to his parents' house. We'd gone down to the basement to jam and hang out like normal. I'd just taken a seat on the sofa when I saw the magazine carefully wedged in between one of the seats.

The cover was of a naked man lounging on some kind of Victorian fainting couch with a blanket positioned carefully over his junk. I'd assumed it was Cindy's as I took it out. I didn't even know what *Gladiator* was before that day but I quickly found out. I opened it, seeing naked or near-naked guys with perfect physiques with every turn of the page.

I gestured to Jack. "What does your sister get up to when we're not around?"

There was a long silence. "Beats me," he finally said as his face turned bright red.

A few days later, I asked Cindy about it. She hadn't told me anything other than telling me over and over it wasn't hers.

"Then whose is it, Cindy?" I'd said. "Jack's?" I'd laughed when I said his name, as if I couldn't believe it.

"You know he's gay, right?" she said after a long silence.

I shook my head.

"He hasn't said anything to you?" She seemed genuinely shocked.

I shook my head again. "He told you?"

Cindy nodded. "Anyways... I've said too much. Let's forget about it."

"Okay..."

"Tom," she said firmly. "I'm serious."

It ended there. I figured Jack would tell me if and when he

was ready. He should have known that it wouldn't change the way I thought of him. Even hearing it straight from his sister, even after the long glances in my direction and the realization that he'd never had a steady girlfriend, I never put two and two together.

Not until the night he kissed me. I'd said something—I don't remember what—that made him laugh. Then he'd leaned in, and it was maybe a few seconds before I processed what was happening and pulled away.

We were still sitting on the sofa, still frozen from what happened. I wanted him to finally be honest about how he felt.

Instead, he started sobbing. The tingle on my lips was still there as I wrapped my arms around him until he stopped crying.

Then, we ordered pizza and found reruns of *The Ed Sullivan Show*. After a certain point he even cracked a smile.

When it was time for me to go, we hugged goodbye.

"You sure you'll be okay on your own?" I asked.

"Yeah. Mom and Dad are getting me in the morning."

My face was tight as I hesitated in his doorway.

"Hey," he said. "I'm sorry again, okay? About, well... you know."

"Take care of yourself," I replied, turning away and descending the stairs, never knowing I'd be turning away from him for the last time.

A NICE MAN my age who's heading to a third shift janitor gig pulls over for me. He reeks of grass, and for the first time, I'm repulsed by the scent. Is this what I smell like?

"How's it going?" he asks.

I sigh. "Could be better, could be worse."

"Yeah, I know how that is," he says.

After a minute or so, I turn my gaze out the window.

"What are you thinking about, man?"

So he's a chatty one. Joy. "The shadows of my past."

The driver laughs, and I make the mistake of asking him where he works.

As if the universe couldn't get any crueler: "Malone's."

All I give him is a "nice" before it's silent for the rest of the drive.

I THINK Cindy always knew how Jack felt about me, and that's why things went south after he left. I've always wondered if my parents knew—or at least suspected—and that's why, no matter what, I'll never be enough for them.

I knew I wasn't gay, but calling Jack my best friend, even my bandmate, always felt like an inaccurate description. Especially after he died, there was no one I could have told about the kiss. Maybe the abruptness of it all is why I ruin things every time I get too close. The only person who knows is Patty. We were sitting in Central Park on a warm day in September when it came up, for maybe our second or third date. And when all she said was "he was lucky to have you" before she smiled and wrapped me in a hug, I knew she was the real deal.

A beautiful angel named Patricia Reilly came into my life and made me believe that I didn't have to be weighed down by my past anymore. I could have it all. I could be the person she was worthy of.

But my past never really left me. It was just waiting to come out to remind me of who I really am. A worthless, pathetic failure that always hurts the ones he loves.

My legs are still lead as I walk up that cobblestone path. I'll call Patty in the morning and tell her everything.

The one good thing Newark had was her. I don't know what I'm going to do without her.

It's my own damn fault.

At least I'll still have the band. I hope. Once I tell them about Malone's, I'm going to have to tell them about Denise. I guess I wasn't thinking that far ahead when I agreed to meet her.

I don't see Donna at first. Sitting on the porch, she's totally silhouetted, but the puff of smoke from her cigarette gives her away.

"Oh," she says. "Sorry. You scared me. You were gone a long time. Where were you?"

I say nothing.

"Be honest with me. Does this have anything to do with when Denise came to the show the other day?"

"I don't really want to talk about it," I say.

"Tom..." Donna trails off. "Look, it's not my business. Actually, scratch that. It is. I've noticed the way Denise looks at you and the way you look at her and I just think that... I don't know. I don't know what's going on, but I think you might need to make some tough decisions."

I realize she's been fighting tears the whole time. I give her a knowing look. I brush some debris off the empty chair next to her and scoot close. "Well, I'm choosing Patty."

"Good," Donna says, drying her eyes. "I love you guys."

"Donna, what exactly happened with Rob?" I ask.

She looks up and makes eye contact with me. "Do you think I'm controlling?"

"No, I don't," I reassure her. "And tell me what's going on? Please?"

"Frank's still inside. I was going to sleep on the couch tonight, but I'm just stalling. Wally agrees that I'm controlling, so I was just wondering if you did, too. That's all," Donna whispers.

"I think you care a lot about this band. And you're passionate and proactive. Those are all good things," I tell her. "But you still haven't answered my question."

Donna sniffles. "Rob propositioned me last week."

Suddenly everything from earlier makes so much more sense.

"He implied that he would be more inclined to extend our contract if I were to go to bed with him. And I said no, of course. I didn't think—" She starts crying, and I rub her back. "I told Frank last week and ever since he's been... I told him I just wanted to keep our heads down and not make a big deal out of it and apparently that makes me controlling."

"You didn't do anything wrong, Donna," I say. "You put your marriage first."

"And I thought we were booked because he believed in our talent," she says, sniffling. "You hear about this stuff happening, but my whole life, this has never—"

"Donna," I say reassuringly. "Deep breaths."

Donna looks at me with glassy eyes and sniffles.

"What about Mila? Have you said anything to her? She was so nice."

Donna shakes her head. "What if she put us up to this because she knew Rob would be interested? 'My spiritual guides specifically called me to mentor a group of four.' I call bullshit."

"I wouldn't assume that," I reason. "She might not know what her brother gets up to."

"It's not worth it. Besides, why would she vouch for me over her own brother?"

"You don't know unless you talk to her," I say.

"I just want to let it go," she says through tears. "I guess this Malone's thing is our last hope, right?"

I have to say something. I force myself to push out the words. "Well, actually, we didn't get it."

She stares. "What? How do you know?"

"Denise told me," I say reluctantly.

"You were with Denise?" Donna says dryly.

"No, not—anyway, I guess Kathy York said something was missing and didn't give her any more detail."

"Okay, great, cool." Donna continues to dry her tears. "All of this for nothing. Awesome. I mean, of course we didn't get it. Why would we?" We sit in silence. "Anyways, Tom. You snuck off to go see Denise?"

My face tightens as I gather my courage. "We kissed. More than just kissed, but—"

Donna wipes tears from her eyes. Her gaze is distant, empty. "I'm really disappointed in you," she whispers.

I didn't think it was possible to hurt any more, but hearing those words come out of her mouth tells me that it is. "Let me finish. I stopped it before it went further. I'm going to tell Patty. Even if it means she leaves me, I owe it to her to say something."

"I see," Donna whispers, not looking at me. "Well, we should probably tell Frank and Wally about Malone's."

Both of them are sitting on the couch as we walk in. Neither says anything, but the window is cracked, and they're both smoking. As soon as Frank and Donna catch eyes, he stands up and the two hug tightly.

"I'm sorry," Donna says.

"I'm sorry too," he replies, rubbing her back and kissing her cheek.

As they pull away from the hug, she looks back at me. "Do you want to tell them the news?"

"We didn't get Malone's," I say. "Officially."

"Oh," Frank says. "How do you know?"

"I was with Denise Peck," I tell them. As hard as it is to go through all of this again, it's not like I have anything left to lose. "She promised news about the audition if we met and we ended up almost having sex."

"Ah," Frank says, barely audibly.

Wally just stares at me.

"Thought you guys ought to know," I say. "In case you still want anything to do with me."

Frank and Wally continue to stare.

"But, I really can't lose you guys, okay?" I continue, fighting tears.

"Who started it?" Frank says.

Donna smacks his shoulder.

"She did, but... I never should have gone. I don't know what I was expecting," I manage, letting tears roll down my cheeks.

"Yeah, what were you expecting?" Frank says dryly.

"I don't know... I..." All of our interactions since the day we met at the Chateau play through my head. Of course she was interested in me.

Of all people, why me?

Because I treated her like a human being?

"He's going to tell Patty when we're back home," Donna tells them.

"Okay," Frank says. "Good luck."

He walks into the room he shares with Donna and slams the door. She follows.

Wally continues to stare me down.

"I stopped it," I tell him.

"For your sake, I really hope she forgives you, but that's more than I'd ever do," he says. After I don't respond, he adds, "I'm going to bed. Night, Tom."

A moment later, I'm alone in the cold, quiet living room.

IN THE MORNING, we book our flights and pack up our belongings. I gather my courage and call Patty once it's all done.

"Hey, Tom," she says. "How's everything?"

"Fine," I say. Hearing her voice is enough to fill me with a rush. "How's Diane?"

"She's okay," Patty says. "*The Wizard of Oz* is on TV, so we're watching. It's a commercial now, so."

I hear Diane's voice in the background.

"She says hi," Patty says.

"Hey," I manage. "I'm going to see you both again soon."

"Really?"

"Yeah, we're coming back tonight," I tell her.

"Oh my gosh," Patty says. "What time? I'll come and get you guys. I'm off today."

I double check our reservations and tell her.

"Sounds good," she says. "Gosh. You should have told me. I haven't been to the house. I've been meaning to clean up."

"Don't worry about it. I can't wait to hold you in my arms, Patty-cake."

"You too. Love you."

"Bye." I hang up and rub my eyes. I'm as in love with her as I was the day we met.

How could I have been so stupid?

I can't tell her. I can't lose her. It was a mistake. We stopped it before it went any further. Besides, I'm never going to see Denise again. So it's not really a big deal.

I know I need to call Dad next. As much as I don't want to, I need to work, especially now that my savings are gone. What I can't stand is knowing I'm going to give him the satisfaction of saying "I told you so." I hold my nose and dial his extension at the store.

"Hello?"

"Hi, it's your son."

"Thomas. Is everything alright?" he asks.

"Tom. It's not that hard, just call me Tom," I say. I've put up with their weird insistence that I'm somehow insulting them by preferring what's always been my nickname—one has to pick and choose their battles after all—but, I don't have the patience for it anymore.

"Okay, *Tom*," he says, his voice dripping with condescension.

Jeez. This is snippy even for him. I know this conversation is going to be rough. Might as well just get it over with. "Just letting you know that we're coming back today. Our other gig ended and Malone's didn't work out," I say.

"I'm sorry to hear that," he says after a beat of dead silence.

He's so flat he'd be laughed out of a middle school drama production. "But it'll be good to have you back. Is there anything else?"

"I would like my job back, please."

"You would like your job back?" Dad repeats. "I'm not sure that's a good idea."

I blink. "What?"

"You ran off and played hooky for a month in LA without any care or regard for the additional work you put on your mother and I. You've shown up to work with a scowl on your face every hour of every day of the week. How do you think that makes us feel? You should be grateful!"

I don't have time for this. A part of me wants to hang up on him now, but it feels like the right time to let a bunch of things off my chest. "For four and a half thousand a year?! I'm *so* grateful. Thanks, Dad."

He says nothing.

"Anyways," I continue, "what do you care about what kind of mood I'm in when I work? You're the one that always taught me that making money is the only thing that matters."

Dad's silence speaks volumes. "What about your last check? Between that and your savings you should be alright for a while," he finally says.

"I don't have my savings," I say. In the past, I would have avoided telling him, but now, I don't care. It's not like I have anything to prove.

"Why don't you have your savings, Thomas?" Dad's voice rises.

"Tom! Just call me Tom!" I yell. Their refusal to do so has never even made sense since he and my brother have always gone by their nicknames, anyways. Why is it okay for them but not for me?

"Sorry, Thomas. It's a little challenging to remember that you reject the name your mother and I gave you."

My eyes roll so hard they could have fallen out of my eye sockets. "Okay, Samuel. Understood. I'd like to hear you and Mom start calling my brother Richard from now on."

"Thomas Alvin Hargrove, cut it out *right now*," Dad says sternly.

Excuse me, am I three years old?

"Frankly, it's none of your business why I don't have my savings!" I yell. Wally, who's just moved his suitcase into the living room, stops and stares. I try to wave him off, but this does nothing. He sits on the couch and watches me for the rest of the call.

"Excuse me?"

"You heard me right," I tell Dad. Getting this all out feels good, and I'm ready to keep going.

"What is the matter with you? And it is my business since you've wasted everything you've earned! That makes me want to hire you back even less!"

"I'm your employee! What the fuck do you care?"

"You're our son! And you'll always be our son!"

"Yeah? Well, what I do with my money stopped being your fucking business when I moved out of the house!" Frank and Donna have entered the living room with their suitcases now, but I'm not done. "Besides, I never asked for the job! You practically forced me to take it!"

"Because you were moping around and feeling sorry for yourself after Jack got killed! You needed to be straightened out!"

I process what he just said on a delay. "You did not just go there."

I hear breathing on the other end of the line.

"Anyways, is it really too much to ask to call me what I prefer to be called?" I say. "And could you show me a little bit of empathy and support? Just for once?"

"We do show you empathy," Dad replies.

"How? When? Give me an example."

"We'll talk about this when you're less upset," Dad snarls. "Have a safe flight back."

I put the phone back on the receiver and scream. Then Donna walks over and starts to rub my shoulder. When I start crying, she brings me into her arms.

"Hey, don't worry about it," she says. "I assume that was Archie Bunker?"

"Who else would it be?" I wail. "He was right. They were always right."

"Tom," Donna starts.

"I can't lose you guys," I plead. "Please, I can't."

"Whoever said we were going anywhere?" Donna says. "We're here for you, always."

"Look," Frank says. "You remember when Donna and I ended things, right?"

I nod. I remember it too well. Except, in their case, there was nothing to the level of what I'd done, just a lot of bad air to go around.

"You were there both for us then, and we're going to be here for you now," Frank says.

"Anyways," Donna says, cutting through the ensuing silence, "fuck Skylark. We don't need them. We'll play in clubs and restaurants until we're old and gray. We'll never record anything for all I care. And we'll prove everyone who told us to quit wrong while we're still standing."

Donna lets me go from her arms and I wipe my tears.

"As far as I'm concerned," Wally says, "I don't care about proving anything to anyone. I love playing music with you guys. I don't care what we do as long as we're together."

"Ditto," Frank says.

"I ditto Frank's ditto," Donna says.

"Yeah," is all I say. "As long as we're together."

We let the last moments in the house linger. When we get back to Newark, this is all going to seem like a bad dream.

side b
Attics of My Life

fourteen

EVERYTHING FEELS lifeless from the moment we touch down at the airport. It doesn't seem right that everything should go back to the way it was before.

I know these ups and downs are a part of life. It seems like life has been mostly downs and I'm tired of holding on for this nebulous day when things are supposed to get better.

Patty picks us up in Frank and Donna's van. She kisses me as I get in the front. I can't help but feel like I don't deserve to touch her.

As we get on the road, it couldn't feel more dark, cold, and gloomy. Six weeks in LA was long enough to make me forget that winter hasn't even started yet. I can't believe that we're staring down the barrel of five months of this, at least. I'm going to be twenty-six in a month and a half, and I have absolutely nothing to show for it.

There's a layer of frost on the ground, and the wind and cloudy, moonless night makes everything so much worse. It's like the weather is taunting us, saying, "See? You can't have what you want. This is what you get for even trying. Who did you think you were?"

"Thank you so much for letting me borrow the van," Patty tells Donna and Frank.

"Don't mention it," Donna says. "You're family."

Patty turns to me. "I was thinking. What do you say we go back to the dealership soon? I may have been once or twice myself."

"We can't," I say, not able to bring myself to look at her.

"What? What do you mean?"

"Dad won't hire me back and there's nothing left in my savings."

"There's nothing left?" she says.

I suddenly become aware of everyone's eyes on us and really wish this conversation was happening in private. "Well, about five dollars, technically. We spent the last of it to get back home."

"I could pitch in," she offers. "For the car."

"I should probably get a job first," I say. "And I don't want just anything. I want the Oldsmobile."

"Forget about it!"

"No!" I say. "That's our car! For us!"

"Technically, it's the dealership's," she says, writhing.

"I can't get a car when I don't know how I'm going to pay rent," I say, staring at the cold, dead landscape around us.

After that, our ride back from the airport is almost entirely silent.

"It was all for nothing," I say right as we pull up to the house.

"No. It wasn't," Patty insists.

"Tom, we'll figure out rent," Donna says as we get out. "It's the least we can do."

"How?" I manage.

No one has anything to say.

"Are you sure that the job is still taken?" I ask Patty. "At the hospital?"

"You'd have to ask Diane, but as far as I know, yes," she says, her tone clipped.

I KNOW from the second that I lay in bed beside Patty, getting a good night's sleep is a wash.

It doesn't take long for her to wrap her arms around me. I give her a tired smile. "Hey."

"Hey. I'm sorry about earlier."

"For what?"

"Pushing you about the car," she says. "You know, I'm not mad about any of it."

"Really?"

"Really." She kisses me. As she reaches her hand down my pants, the memory of Denise on my lap flashes through my mind. I have to pull away.

"What is it?" she asks.

"Nothing," I whisper, rolling over onto my back. "I'm tired."

She seems to understand. For now, I let her lay her head on my shoulder.

I drift in and out of consciousness. The moments I'm in spur mixed feelings. Patty's sound asleep against my shoulder. When we were apart, I didn't realize how much I missed her beside me. Not until just now. I can't stop thinking about

Denise, the things I haven't said, and the fact that I need a job. Even if the others are going to use their nonexistent money to help me out, I'm not going to take charity from anyone. There is something that comes to mind almost immediately. I don't know what anyone else is going to say, but I'm not going to get involved. It will be a working relationship. That's all.

THAT MORNING, I wait for everyone else to leave for work before I catch the bus to the other side of town. On the ride over, the thought crosses my mind that there's a very real chance Cindy might not be there anymore. If that ends up being the case, I'll forget about it and I'll start over. But I have to try.

I stare out the windows at the bleary scene, thinking that Jack was only a part of the reason why things went south with me and Cindy. It was the fall she took off the uneven bars in Philly a few months after he left. She came back to Newark with a broken leg, but it took a while to sink in that she'd never compete again.

I'm shaking the moment I get off the bus. I've been to this side of town every now and again, but only if I have to and never for very long. It's scary how easily it all comes back, like no time passed at all. I pass the intersection where Jack and I hitched to catch the Doors concert in New York and the bodega Cindy and I used to stop at in the mornings. There's the newsstand where I first broke down and she held me in her arms after she told me that Jack was dead.

The cold keeps me alert as I walk three blocks down Rose Street, and another down Iris. Then, I see it. The blue roof.

The shutters. 1951. And her rusted Pinto in the driveway. Is it still running after all this time?

I take a deep breath as I walk up the chipped wood steps onto the stoop.

As I'm about to knock, I realize that this is a terrible idea. *What am I thinking?* Am I really about to beg my ex-girlfriend for a job after she betrayed me by sleeping with my friend—the one who saved our lives and livelihoods after Jack died?

Yes, I am.

I don't know what else to do.

This is just for now. It's going to be okay.

I ring the doorbell.

Nothing happens.

I ring it again. Still nothing.

I suddenly remember that the bell is probably still broken.

I knock.

Nothing.

I knock again.

I hear a familiar voice yelling at someone from down the hall. My heart thumps. It's her. And him.

I knock a third time.

"Jesus fucking Christ, Grant! How am I supposed to hear shit with you yelling in my ear all the time?!" she yells.

My face tightens as I see her open the door. Cindy. She looks... good. Still stick thin, but good. Her ash-blonde hair is long and looks like it's been teased. There's actually some color in her face. Her clothes, an argyle sweater and corduroy pants, have been ironed. I take in the presence of the first woman I ever loved. It was so easy to forget how important she'd once been to me, to keep that part of my life down, but suddenly I'm a fifteen-year-old boy again.

I notice the ring on her finger and my face gets even tighter. It irritates me in a way I can't fully describe to think that Grant, of all people, straightened her out.

She looks at me like I'm a ghost. I realize she's holding a pack of cigarettes in her hand as she steps out and joins me on the porch.

"Tom," Cindy gasps. Her voice is still raspy as she looks me up and down. "You're a wreck. What's going on?"

"It's good to see you too," I mutter.

"How long has it been?"

"About four years, give or take," I tell her. "I need your help."

She lights her cigarette and gestures the box towards me. I shake my head. She brings it to her lips, and I watch the smoke curl out and fade into the air. "I know, I know," she says once she has a moment. "I'm trying to quit."

I say nothing.

"Why do you need my help?" she says flatly.

"I'm out of a job," I say.

"Oh," Cindy says, understanding. "We've given all of that up."

"Really?"

"Yeah," Cindy says. "You haven't?"

I'm frozen right there on her porch.

"Still trying to make the music thing happen, huh?"

"I don't know," I whisper. "Sort of."

"It's good you kept up with it," she says. "Are you playing solo?"

I shake my head. "No, I'm in a band. They needed a bassist, and I didn't sell my car to get that for nothing."

Cindy smiles tiredly. "Right. I still can't believe you did that. It was kind of awesome, though. Sticking it to your folks."

"It really wasn't," I say. Seven years since I'd gotten rid of the Datsun to get my own bass. Jack's one that I'd been borrowing all that time was on the fritz anyway. I thought it was going to open up doors for us and I'd get a new car in no time. Instead, I played two gigs with it before Jack was drafted. "The bass was collecting dust until recently."

"Why'd you never sell it back?" Cindy says.

"It wouldn't have been worth it. I can live without a car. I can't live without music."

Cindy smiles. "Tell you what. We might be able to help you. But this"—she gestures at the space between us—"it's not gonna happen."

"Okay," I say. "I'm spoken for, so."

"Are you now?"

I nod, clenching my jaw as I do.

She watches me and after a moment, takes a step towards the door. She opens it and yells down the hall. "Hey, Grant! Get out here!"

I gulp.

He looks the same, too. His dark hair is still just as oily, and he's got a mustache now. He sees me and smiles. "Tom. Good to see you!" He gives me a hug, which I have to carefully pull away from. I don't know what I was expecting but it wasn't for him to act like we were all still the best of friends.

"Tom needs work," Cindy mutters.

"Yeah, I run a furniture store now. We opened about a year ago. Can you lift up to a hundred pounds?"

"Sure," I say.

"We need people to do deliveries. Mostly around here, but sometimes into New York, too."

"What are the hours?"

"As many as you want," he says.

"Full forty?"

"Sure."

He runs back into the house to get a card with the address and info. He hands it to me. "You start tomorrow. Eight o'clock. Don't be late."

"Noted."

I'm about to turn around to leave when Cindy looks to me. "How'd you get here?"

I hesitate before telling her the truth.

"Where are you living these days? Let me drive you back."

"So, you must really be desperate to want to come to me," Cindy says once we're on the road.

I don't reply.

"You know, it's funny because I was just thinking about you," she says.

"Were you now?"

"Well, we're coming up to the anniversary," she says, inhaling deeply. I see her eyes are watery. "Mom died a year ago and with Dad's MS..."

Eliza is dead? I can't remember the last time I'd seen her or Scott—they always insisted I call them by their first names—but it must have been sometime in the haze that was 1972. They'd never been anything but kind, treating me more like I thought parents should treat their kids than my actual ones ever had. And Scott's one of the most positive people I've ever met. He was always so full of energy.

"Anyway, Dad's gotten a lot worse, so, there's that."

I'm so sorry to hear that, Cindy," I finally manage. "How did she—"

"Pancreatic cancer," she says dryly.

I give her an empathetic look.

"Anyway, I was just thinking," Cindy continues, "it just makes me think about how short life is. That's why we're giving up selling, me and Grant. We want to have a family before it's too late, you know? And, um... I'm a little past running from the cops and from wondering if I ruined someone's life to make a quick buck."

I look out at the bleak city street. It's not something I like to think about often, but with Cindy now, I'm forced to reflect. We never got caught, even after I ended up in the hospital, but things easily could have gone a different way. "Right."

"But, I'm happy with Grant... you found someone... Anyway, I guess what I'm trying to say is that I think everything happens for a reason."

I know this is the closest I'm ever going to get to an apology from her. That's okay. It's all I really need.

We've pulled up to the house by then.

"Anyway," she says, "see ya."

When I walk back inside the solitary house, I flop onto my bed, wondering if I've made a terrible mistake. Still, I don't know how that could be. The others know Cindy and Grant by name but not by face. Only my family does. I can just tell them that I got a job. I can't imagine why the rest would ever come up.

That night, when everyone gets home, I tell them the news.

They accept my story—that I was walking down the street, saw the ad, went in, and was hired on the spot.

FOR THE REST of the year, I really think everything's going to be okay. The job—if I can disassociate enough from the circumstances—is okay. It pays me less than even my parents did, but I at least don't want to kill myself every hour of the day. We have enough to get by, and that's what matters.

The band never makes a conscious decision to take a break, but it ends up just sort of happening. Donna's print shop is in the busy season because of the holidays. While Frank's office completely bought his excuse about being in the Philippines, he's still on thin ice for taking so much time off. Meanwhile, Baskin-Robbins cut Wally's hours for the winter months, so he has to focus his energy on finding another job.

"Hey," he asks me one night at dinner. "Do they need any more people at the furniture shop?"

"Not right now," I lie. "Sorry." In fact, we're understaffed. I hate to lie to Wally like that, but I figure he's resourceful enough, and I can't risk anyone finding out how I got this job.

The second week of November, Patty and I receive an invitation from my parents for Thanksgiving dinner.

We talk about it in the living room one night after she gets home from a shift. "You're invited, too? What's gotten into them?"

"Tom, they're trying their best," she says.

"Are they really?" I shoot back.

"When's the last time you've seen or talked to them?" she asks me.

"Since my dad refused to let me have my job back," I say.

"Well, to be fair—"

"There's no to be fair, Patty! Why are you taking their side?"

Patty takes a deep breath. "You never know—"

I'm really not in the mood for this. "Newsflash? Your parents and mine are *not* the same. Just because yours were wonderful, that shouldn't mean I have to suffer in front of people who hate my guts!"

Patty scoffs. "What the hell is wrong with you?"

I say nothing.

"You've been off ever since you got back and I don't really know why." Patty inhales. "I know the trip didn't go the way you wanted it to but that's not on me."

"Patty, I'm sorry," I say. I reach for her hand, but she pulls back.

"Is it your new job?" she finally says.

Sort of. It's not just that, but also Denise and what happened that night. No matter how many times I try to forget it, it's a bug crawling in the back of my brain. That's what I want to say to her. "I don't really want to talk about it," I mutter.

Patty sighs. "Why not? You know, you can tell me anything." She reaches her hand towards mine, which I slowly take.

Here goes nothing. "Remember about how I told you I met Denise Peck and we went to a party at her house?"

Patty nods.

I squeeze her hand tightly. "We got close."

"Okay..."

"I thought she needed a friend." I pause again, wondering

if I can really go through with telling her all of this. But I'm too far into stop now.

"And?" Patty says.

"She made a pass at me."

Patty laughs. I'm not sure what reaction I was expecting, but it wasn't this.

"What?"

"That's what you've been so up in arms about? Did you make a pass at her?"

"No. I mean, she knew all about you from the beginning, so. I told her I wasn't interested."

"So what's the big deal?" Patty says with a laugh.

"I guess the others thought it was obvious she had a crush on me and I ignored them, so."

"Tom," Patty says, laughing again. "Just forget about it." She leans forward and kisses me. "I love you."

"I love you too," I mutter.

If only that's all that it was. But I can't bring myself to push it any further, especially as I apologize for the comment I made about her parents. Maybe that's all she needs to know. Maybe it's for the best we just move on.

WE END up getting out of spending Thanksgiving with my parents on the condition that we'll be there for Christmas. This is perfectly reasonable as it gives me a little bit more time to cool down. I'm still too furious to be in the same room as them.

Instead, the five of us drive to Pennsylvania to spend a week with the Rices. I know they're not a huge fan of how Wally's still scooping ice cream and exerting all of his energy on The

Hermits when he could be going to law school instead or something. But they've been nothing but nice for as long as I've known them, and I've always got the impression that they respect the fact that he's an adult and can make his own decisions about what he wants to do with his life.

It's a nice, relaxing trip. Mrs. Rice tells us over and over again that we're special guests in her bed-and-breakfast, and it's her turn to take care of us because we've all worked so hard. We still manage to pitch in where we can, though. There's good food, good company, some time outdoors and no judgement for once—but like all good things, it's over by the time we blink.

As the weeks pass, we all go to work, we come home, we eat, we try to relax. Rinse, repeat. Diane's condition seems to stabilize, at least, for now. As the temperatures drop and the snow begins to fall, it's crazy how little it takes for our time in LA to feel like a haze.

Those were false memories.

This is our life.

Day by day, we survive.

fifteen

"Tom, I have a surprise for you," Patty says when I get home from work on December 15th, three days before my birthday. She's smiling and tells me to sit.

I find my way to the couch as she disappears into the hallway.

My birthday. It's Sunday. I hadn't even thought about it.

She comes back and sits down next to me with an envelope. Then, she kisses me. "Open it."

I do. There's $150 in cash and a postcard of a restaurant with gorgeous views of New York City. "windows on the world," it says. "world trade center, manhattan, nyc."

I flip the card over. There's a handwritten note from Gracie.

Tom- Had a gig shooting here and they treated us to dinner afterwards- thought you'd enjoy for your birthday. We wanted it to be a surprise and reservations fill up fast so we've got you and Patty down for 7:30. Thought you could enjoy the city, too.

Have fun, kids!

Love,
Diane and Gracie

I gape at the money and look back at Patty.

"It's for dinner and a hotel so we can have a staycation," she explains.

"They didn't have to give this much!" I exclaim.

"They wanted to do it," she says. She leans in and kisses me again. "I love you."

"I love you, too."

I really don't deserve her.

I WAKE up on my birthday to a fresh snowfall. Patty's not beside me, but I smell coffee coming from down the hall and realize it's because everyone's already woken up. I smile as I remember everyone's off work today. I hear their voices and them in the kitchen. They're all in their pajamas, drinking coffee, relaxing and standing around the pot. They all see me and start singing "Happy Birthday."

By the end of it, Patty pours me a cup. It's my Superman one.

"Washed this for you," she says, handing it to me with a kiss.

"Thanks, guys," I say, holding back tears.

"We love you, Tom," Donna says.

"Some of the time," Frank says, teasing.

"You really changed our lives," Donna says. She's fully crying. "I'm so happy we picked you up and gave you a ride to the Dead concert that day."

I set my coffee cup down, step forward and give her a hug. "I'm glad you were there to give me a ride."

When we pull away from the hug, everyone's still staring at me. "Gosh, you guys, you're acting like I'm terminally ill."

"Shut up and let us celebrate you," Frank says, tapping my shoulder. He and Wally finish their coffee and announce they're going to go outside to shovel.

After they leave, Patty looks to me with a smile. "I'm making French toast and bacon. It's still your favorite, right?"

"Anything you make is my favorite," I tell her.

She blushes.

"Sure you don't need help, Pats?" Donna asks her.

"Sure." Patty keeps her eyes on me as she smiles.

"I'm going to start my LA screen print," Donna tells us. "The trip had to have been good for something." She waves at us. "I'll be in the living room."

I approach Patty, stroking her cheek with my free hand before leaning in to give her a kiss.

"What?"

"I love you," I tell her.

"I love you, too."

.   .   .

PATTY and I leave for our dinner reservation in Manhattan that afternoon. I'm in my favorite green-and-blue shirt and corduroys. She put on my favorite dress of hers, her blue velvet one. I sing the first part of "Blue Velvet" when I see her.

"Shut up," she says with a blush. "You know I love this dress."

"I do too."

Something shifts as soon as we transfer onto the subway. As we watch the skyscrapers roll by from the train car window, the vibe is different. A weight's been lifted off. Suddenly, I don't feel bad. The constant, gray cloud that follows me in Newark always magically seems to disappear when I'm not there.

Maybe I should pay attention to that.

Patty slips her hand into mine and puts her head on my shoulder as we watch the city at dusk roll by. "I could get used to living here," she whispers.

I nod and wrap my arm around her. I'd love to live here, too, but it feels so out of reach.

"You're awfully quiet," Patty whispers.

I give her a smile as I slide my hand into hers.

She looks at me tiredly and puts her head on my shoulder.

"HAVE you ever been up this high?" Patty asks me once we're in the elevator of the World Trade Center's North Tower.

"The Empire State Building, once," I tell her. "When Rick and I were little. You know that."

"This is even higher," a gray-haired man standing next to us says. We look and see his wife beside him. They're both smiling at us.

"It's his birthday," Patty tells them.

"Let me guess. Eighteen," the husband says with a grin.

"Twenty-six," I say, blushing.

He turns back to his wife. "Were we that young once, dear?"

"I think so."

My breath is taken away as soon as we enter. Floor-to-ceiling windows, flanked by the tower's metal beams, present the city below us. Its lights twinkle like millions of tiny stars in the night sky. Suddenly I understand the name. It literally feels like we're on top of the world.

The restaurant is busy as the older couple approaches the booth first.

I hear the host say, "We've got your window table right there."

The wife turns around. "They can have it."

Patty and I blink. "Are you sure?" she asks.

"Of course," the husband says. "We can take theirs."

A moment later, they've switched our reservations. We would have been at one of the far tables. The views would have been gorgeous no matter where in the restaurant we would have been, but still, the window table we get makes this day even better. I find myself wanting to thank the older couple and at least find out their names, but by then, they're out of sight.

As we scan menus, neither of us say much. We just smile at each other. She really is so beautiful. I don't know why I ever indulged Denise's attraction to me.

"What?" she finally says, blushing.

"You look really beautiful in that dress."

Her cheeks turn red.

"You always look beautiful."

Patty leans in close to me. "If you're nice, I'll let you take it off later," she whispers.

A rush floods through me. We haven't had sex since I've been back. Not by design, but I haven't been in the mood, mostly because I don't know how I could touch her after what I did.

Now's the time for all of that to change.

I take her hand, kiss it and smile.

THE NEXT MORNING, I awake in our hotel room to the sun and Patty still curled up against me. I sit up, stretch and rub my eyes, thinking that was the best night of sleep I've had in a long time. Last night sure helped, too.

She wakes up a second after I do. She sits up, slides into my arms, and we kiss.

We have a little money left over from Diane and Gracie, so we order room service.

If only it could always be like this.

sixteen

THE NEXT NIGHT, we're back in Newark, and all of us have an early Christmas celebration at the house. It's not much, but Donna makes cinnamon rolls and eggnog. Since Wally's going to Pennsylvania and Donna and Frank will be in Delaware to spend time with Donna's parents, Patty and I will have the house to ourselves until the 26th.

It's about -5 degrees outside as we all sit around the table. At first, we have the radio on until we hear the opening notes of "We've Only Just Begun." And then, a syrupy female voice —not Karen Carpenter—singing the opening line. Next, instead of "to live," she sings "to shop" as a male joins her.

All of us exchange a look.

This is the Malone's jingle?

It's a fucking riff.

Frank stands up and turns it off. He goes to our record collection and puts on *The Beach Boys' Christmas Album.* "To help us think warm thoughts," he says.

He sits back down. Instead of "Little Saint Nick," "We

Three Kings Of Orient Are" plays. "Frank, this is the wrong fucking side," I say.

Donna gives me a glare first, followed by Patty and Wally. Frank just sits there.

I regret saying anything, especially as the song reverberates through the room like a message from God himself. "Sorry. Leave it on."

I close my eyes and Patty squeezes my hand.

"Hey," Frank says after a while. "It's been a bit since we've played."

"It has," Wally remarks.

"We should change that," Donna says. "I'm feeling the itch to get back into things."

"Me too," I say. The thought of playing again with all of them is invigorating.

"New Years resolution?" Frank says.

"I'm in!" I announce. I look around at all of them. The warmth of contentment spreads through my body.

I DON'T KNOW why I'm surprised when it all comes crashing down. Of course it does, because I can't do anything without it coming back to bite me in the ass.

On Christmas, Patty's in a terrible mood, and she won't tell me why. She's been in one ever since I got home from work the night before.

"Is it something I said or did?" I ask a million times.

"No," she repeats.

"Is it my parents?" I try.

"No." Finally, she says, "let's just get ready and go over, okay?"

She barely says a word to me on the entire bus ride. As we're all sitting in the living room, she becomes thoroughly engaged in a conversation with Jenny and pretends like I'm not even there.

As we all eat dinner, I'm thinking about how I'm going to confront her when Mom says, "Thomas, you'll never believe who I ran into yesterday!"

"Who did you run into, Mom?" I ask.

"Cindy!" she exclaims.

"Oh. Okay."

Patty turns to me, her face white.

"She said you're working for her husband now. That you came to her because you were desperate for work. Why didn't you tell us?"

"I... uh..." I start. "Well, I needed something in a pinch, so."

From the look on Patty's face, I know I'm about to have it as soon as we're alone.

"She seems like she's doing well," Mom says, her tone chipper. I don't know if she's oblivious to what she's done or if she knows and doesn't care.

"How's the job going?" Dad asks.

"It's fine," I say.

"No interpersonal conflicts getting in the way?" he says condescendingly.

I shake my head.

"Good," he remarks. Then, they change the subject.

Suddenly, I can't eat anymore.

A short time later, as it's time for us to go, Patty whispers in my ear, "Hey, Tom, we're getting a cab. We need to talk."

Shitfuckshit.

This is going to be bad.

I BARELY HAVE time to take off my coat before she slams the door.

Somehow, I find my way to the couch as she tosses off her coat and stands in front of me, her arms crossed. "So. I wasn't going to say anything because I wanted to have a nice Christmas, and I kept telling myself I was overreacting. It's fine. It's not that big of a deal. It's not like anything really happened—"

"Just say what you have to say," I rush out.

"I'm getting there!" Patty shrieks. "You didn't turn down Denise's pass, did you?"

My face goes white. I can't bring myself to look at her. "What?"

"She called me."

My entire body goes white in an instant.

"How does she even have our phone number?"

"I—"

Patty repeats her question. Still, I stumble over my words.

"I want an answer!"

"She probably... her husband works at Skylark where we auditioned so I'm sure she probably got that from... I don't know. What did she say?" *Oh God, Denise, what the actual fuck?*

"That she had feelings for you and she was selfish to only think about what she wanted and not about me. That you're a really good person... 'love is a beautiful thing' or some garbage. She wanted me to forgive her. She was very drunk... so... what happened? The truth this time."

The words don't come.

"What did she want me to forgive her for, Tom?"

"We kissed," I say.

"And?"

"Just kissed," I repeat.

Patty scoffs. "You sure it wasn't more than that?"

I see a flash of Denise's half-naked body again. "No. Not all the way. I stopped before it got that far."

"Uh-huh," Patty says, crossing her arms, stifling tears and looking away. "You had the chance to tell me and you didn't. But you told Donna, didn't you?!"

"What?"

"Before they left, she was all, 'oh, you and Tom worked it out then?' I was really confused but now everything makes so much sense."

I have absolutely nothing to say for myself.

"So, Donna knew?" Patty says.

I nod.

"Did you tell Frank and Wally?"

I nod again.

Patty scoffs. "Great. So everyone knew that my boyfriend kissed another woman except for me."

All I can do is bury my face in my hands.

"If you'd just told me, we could have worked through it together. It really hurts that you would lie about something like this." She has to take a minute to catch her breath and stifle tears. *This can't be happening.* Eventually, I look up as she finds her way to a sit, but she keeps her distance from me.

"When did Denise call you?" I manage.

"Yesterday. When you were at work. For your ex-girlfriend," she snips.

"I don't work for her, I work for her husband," I correct.

"So do you really move furniture or are you selling drugs?" she demands.

"I move furniture!" I yell.

"Whatever."

An agonizingly long silence follows.

"Don't you have anything to say for yourself?" Patty eventually says, keeping her gaze downwards.

"What do you want me to say?"

"You could have *at least* told me about Cindy," Patty says, "instead of lying!"

"Patty..." I start. I try to take her hand, but she shirks away.

"I'm going to go stay with Diane and Gracie for a little bit," Patty says. "I don't know how long. I'm going to leave first thing in the morning."

"Are we..." I can't bring myself to say the words "breaking up."

"I don't know. I just need space, okay?"

"How long?"

"I need space. I'll let you know when I'm ready to talk to you again."

Without another word, she leaves and slams the door. I have a few minutes alone in the cold and empty living room before I realize all of my pajamas are in our room. After I swallow my pride and knock, she tosses a pair out of the door.

I don't get a wink of sleep that night. All I can think about is how badly I want to trip. I don't want to take stuff from the others without asking, and my stash—which I have saved for a rainy day, so to speak—is under our bed.

I pretend to be asleep when Patty leaves the house at six in the morning.

When I'm sure she's gone, I get up and check for my stash.

I have more acid and speed left than I thought. I hold off for now and take my grass into the living room and smoke it.

I'm not sure how long I've been sitting there by the time Frank and Donna come back.

"Happy Boxing Day!" Frank exclaims.

I don't register him right away.

"Lovebirds, are you there?" he continues. His words rub salt into my wound.

Donna sees me then and points to Frank, her face grim.

"Tom, what's wrong?" she asks.

"Patty's gone!" I wail.

Donna and Frank exchange a look. She sets her stuff down. He takes everything into their room as she goes to sit next to me.

"What happened?" she asks.

"Denise called our house and told Patty about the kiss," I say between sobs.

"You never told her yourself?" Donna asks, confused.

I shake my head.

As I break down, Donna takes me into her arms. "Tom, what happened? You were supposed to talk to her."

"I was too scared." I barely get the words out through my sobs. "I couldn't stand the thought of losing her."

"Is she gone, gone?"

"She went to stay with Diane." I'm still high, so everything around me moves in slow motion. "She needs space."

"Okay," Donna says calmly. "Then give her that. It's going to be okay."

"Is it?"

"I'm sorry this is happening."

"That's not all," I say. As I tell her about how I went to

Cindy, too, and that's how I got the job with Grant, she looks at me but says nothing. "I went because I thought they'd help me sell. I didn't know what else to do."

She still doesn't speak.

"Donna, I swear, it was all a big mistake," I sob.

"Tom. Deep breaths. Just take it one day at a time."

OVER THE NEXT FEW DAYS, the others act like they're not avoiding me when they so obviously are. I sense it from the dinners they have without me, the quiet stares when I come home from work, and the conversations that abruptly end when I enter the room.

On December 29th, Rick calls the house when I'm home alone and asks if Patty and I have any plans for New Years.

"I don't," I say. "Not sure about Patty."

"Well, if you don't, I was going to say that you two are welcome to come spend it with Jenny and I. I'm having some friends from the office over. Did you ever meet Jerry? From the office?"

"Maybe. I'm not sure," I say. "His name's Jerry?"

"Yeah, he's in accounts with me, super cool," Rick says. "Tom and Jerry! I can't believe I've never introduced you two!"

"Rick, Patty's gone," I finally manage.

"*What?*" he exclaims. "What's the matter? What happened?"

"I'm not sure if she's coming back," I say. "I cheated on her."

"Um... Tom? You're pulling my leg, right?"

"No, I'm not." Somehow, I manage to spit out the entire Denise story. I know Rick's always liked her, so I have no idea how he's going to react. I still hear his breathing on the other end when I add, "By the way. Mom and Dad can *never* know about this. I'm serious. I'll never hear the end of it."

"Why? Because of Patty or because of Denise?" Rick finally says.

"Both."

"You ended it before anything happened, right?" he asks.

"Right."

"I guess I don't know what to say," he replies.

"Say that your big brother is a worthless fuckup? I can take it."

"No, I'm not going to say that, because it's not true," Rick says.

"Then why do Mom and Dad act like it is? What do you guys talk about when I'm not around?"

Rick scoffs. "Believe it or not, you're not the only topic of conversation that comes up. Mom and Dad worry about you because they care."

"Oh, and you can stop being condescending to me too," I snap. "I'm over the constant self-righteousness because you're their favorite."

"Tom, I'm about to hang up this phone right now," Rick says. "There's no need to get mad at me. None of what you're going through right now is my fault."

I say nothing.

"I'm worried about you," he continues. "Are you—"

"What? A danger to myself?" I snap. "I'm fine. So, you can piss off and stop worrying."

I hang up the phone.

. . .

FRANK, Donna and Wally finally let me back into their circle on New Years Eve. We ring in 1978 by watching the ball drop on TV and not doing too much of anything else. Close to midnight, I go under my bed to get my stash—only to discover it isn't there anymore.

I ask Donna and she pretends to be clueless.

I probe again in the morning, at breakfast. She admits she took it.

"Why would you do that?" I demand.

"Look, I spoke to your brother," she says.

"Rick called you?" My face is pale. When I confided in him about what was going on, I didn't think he'd do this.

"Yes, he did. He's worried about you. He said you got really bad, ended up in the hospital and almost died after Jack—"

Fucking hell, Rick. Of course. "That was a long time ago," I reason. In those days I'd been so strung out all the time that I only barely remember it myself.

"Tom, I know you too well. Your stash is going to be hidden in a place where you can't find it."

GRANT FINALLY CATCHES onto the fact that something's up at the end of my second week back at work.

After he probes, I reluctantly tell him what's going on with Patty. I tell him I cheated with someone I met in LA, but I don't go into much more detail than that.

"Oh, yeah, that's rough," Grant says. "At the end of the day, she's your girl. The one you go home to. That's what matters, right?"

I nod vaguely. *Wonderful advice, Grant. Thank you.*

"Cindy was my girl once," I tell him. "The one I went home to."

He stares at me with a blank, tight look. "Hey... for what it's worth... there's no excuse for how we went about it—"

"You just couldn't wait to break it to me gently?" I say, half-sarcastically.

"I hated hurting you. It's just that—"

"What?"

"Buddy, you were hard to reach. Your brain was somewhere else and Cindy was worried about you. She came to me. One thing led to another—"

"Alright, I get it," I say, looking away at the bleak late afternoon sky.

"I had sort of hoped that you coming to us meant things have been forgiven," Grant says. I look at the weary expression on his face. He's earnest about this.

"Sure, Grant," I say tiredly.

"Hey, Cindy's cooking some dinner," he offers. "We'd be happy to have you."

"Cindy's cooking? Lord, help us," I say.

Grant laughs. "What's wrong with her cooking?"

"Has she figured out how to not burn things by now?"

Grant stares at me blankly. "Did she ever not know?"

"Never mind," I say. So Grant inspired her to be a better cook, too. Noted. "I'd love to." That's going to be a fun conversation to have with Patty when she and I eventually do talk again. But I'm so lonely. At home, all I can think of is the gaping hole left by her absence.

. . .

WHILE IT's odd to be in the house Cindy and I once shared, a helping of grass helps me dissociate.

Dinner is spaghetti and meatballs with marinara sauce, garlic bread, and salad. It's not the best I've ever tasted, but it doesn't need to be. This exact spread used to be a Newsom family specialty, one I had many helpings of over the years.

"Your mom's recipe?" I ask as Cindy sits down and we start to eat.

Cindy nods. "It was in her stuff, and I thought, I'm finally ready to try."

I smile. From my first bites, I'm filled with a familiar sort of warmth, one that reminds me of a time long before I knew the names Patty Reilly, Wally Rice, Frank Santos, Donna Byrne, and hermits were people who lived alone, away from the world.

As we're cleaning up, Grant excuses himself to go outside for a smoke.

I stare at Cindy with a raised eyebrow once he's gone.

"I know, I know. We're trying. It's not that easy." She hesitates, and then purses her lips. "I found something else when I was cleaning out. Can I show you?"

"What is it?"

In response, Cindy gets up, disappears down the hallway, and returns a moment later with a crumpled, paper record sleeve.

My heart skips a beat as I realize what this is.

My hands shake as she hands it to me, confirming my suspicions.

MONSTER MASH

"A WORLD WITHOUT LOVE"

Abbott and Costello, obviously, was taken, but Cindy's suggestion hadn't been lost on us when we were deciding on a name. We were led to Monster Mash through *Abbott and Costello Meets Frankenstein,* and it fit. Scott and Eliza had booked the recording session as a present for Jack's seventeenth birthday. They had two versions made—one for me, one for him. In the depths of my grief, I'd snapped mine in two, something I've regretted every day since. I never even stopped to think his still existed.

"I was going to listen to it," Cindy starts. "But I—"

"Put it on," I say.

As she does, I close my eyes and prepare myself for the flood of memories.

The record is scratchy, and Jack was a worse singer than I remember. But it's his voice. This stupid little record born out of a pipe dream—it's made him immortal.

"I think I messed things up with my girlfriend," I say about halfway through the song. I don't even try to stop the tears that are rolling down my cheeks.

Cindy laughs dryly. "Really? I'm shocked."

I give her a look. "How do I fix it?"

"By being you," she says.

"I seem to remember that not working out too well," I reply.

"We were bad for each other," Cindy says. "But I think we both always knew that. And you can be a pain in the neck, but you are also generous and kind and so loyal to the people you love. That's a rare quality, and it's going to take you far. I didn't know how to express it at the time, but I've always known that about you. It's why I loved you. It's why Jack loved you, too."

I look at her and see she's crying too. "Thanks," I whisper.

"I'm really glad you came to us," Cindy says. "I didn't think I'd ever see you again. So, thank you. It's been nice."

I give her a tired nod, and we listen to the rest of the song in silence. She takes the record out and puts it back in the sleeve. "Do you want it?"

I nod, and she hands it to me.

A few moments later, Grant comes back in and says he'll take me home.

I give Cindy a hug before we go.

"Don't get too carried away," she says with a laugh.

I can't help but smile. Some things don't change.

A FEW DAYS LATER, it's still been radio silence from Patty, and I'm going crazy. I try calling the apartment and Gracie answers.

"Is Patty there?" I ask.

"Yeah, she's here," Gracie says dryly. She calls to Patty, and I hear the slightest wisp of her voice in the background. "She can't talk to you right now."

"Come on, two minutes."

Breathing.

"One?"

"I'm with a client, Tom." She hangs up the phone.

If Patty wants to break up with me, she should just say so. Living through this limbo is torture. Still, I try to do my best to respect her boundary.

After another few days, I'm home alone, and I can't take it anymore. I call again. Diane answers.

"What do you want?" she says impatiently.

"Please don't hang up," I plead. "Can you at least pass along a message?"

"Tom, I'm extremely fucking exhausted right now. Make it quick."

My brain is fried from a combination of exhaustion and the fact that I really need a fix as I start.

"Tell her that I miss her and I understand that she doesn't want to talk to me, but it's been three weeks... if she wants to break up, that's fine. I just want her to know that I messed up really bad and there's not a day that goes by where I don't think about what I did. I'm sorry I didn't tell her about Denise—"

"Oh, yeah, Denise your landlady?" Diane cuts in.

My heart skips a beat. I'd completely forgotten about that, and I'm even more ashamed I lied to Diane, too.

"I was afraid to lose her," I continue. "Going to Cindy, I was so desperate, like you wouldn't believe. As much as I selfishly want her to give me another chance, I'm thinking that she deserves so much better than me."

"Probably," Diane remarks.

How far I've fallen since she was asking me to propose to Patty only a few months ago. I continue. "I hope she has a great life. Anyways... meeting her... and you, and Gracie... was the best thing that's ever happened to me. I love her. I always will."

"I will pass the message on," Diane says in a monotone. "Goodbye, Tom." She hangs up.

As I put the phone back in the receiver, everything around me freezes. I don't have a chance to process before I feel a rush of cold air and realize that Wally's eyes are on me. He's just finished taking off his shoes. He stares me down before slamming the front door.

"What the hell, man?" he says.

"What the hell, what?" I reply.

He approaches me, showing me a piece of a flyer he tore off. "O&P Furniture Supply? That's you, right?"

"Yeah." I inspect the paper.

HELP WANTED

"Something must have changed—"

"I don't believe you," he says. "And even if that were true, why wouldn't you tell me? You know I need a job."

I say nothing.

"If you don't want to work together, that's fine. I know you're going through it, but don't lie to me."

He disappears down the hall and I hear a door slam. I follow behind him and knock.

"Wally—" I start.

"Fuck off," he says.

This can't be real life.

I just want it all to stop.

I want to wake up from this nightmare. Or at least numb my brain to it all.

My stash. It's got to be somewhere in the house.

I'm not sure how long I spend looking, but I end up tearing apart Donna's closet before I find it in bags at the bottom of one of her bins. It's all there. Thank God.

I take them out and go into my room. I get a glass and pour myself a bit of whiskey.

Next, I take the speed. After I've had enough, I lay down on the bed and let it take hold.

seventeen

WHEN I COME TO, the first thing I become aware of is fluorescent lights. The second thing is the beeping of hospital machines.

My head hurts like hell.

I see Mom first. We lock eyes, and she vigorously shakes Dad out of a nap.

"Thomas," she says, scooting her chair closer and stroking my forehead. "Oh, God."

I try to wrack my brain. I don't remember much after I found my speed in Donna's room, only that I didn't want to keep fighting this battle anymore. "What happened?"

"You were high as a kite—" Mom says.

"Mary Beth," Dad cuts in, scooting forward and taking her hand. He turns to me now. "Your friend found you."

"My friend?"

"One of them," Dad says.

"What was their name?"

As Dad gives me a blank stare, another wave of pain hits me like a hammer to the head.

"Willy?" Mom says.

"Wally?"

"I don't know," she replies.

"Did he have blond hair?"

"Yes, he did," Mom says after a beat.

"That's Wally," I reply, my tone sharp.

"Don't talk to your mother that way," Dad says condescendingly.

"Oh, jeez, I'm sorry. I've only known them for over three years. It's not like we're in a band or live together or anything."

Mom gives me an exasperated look and turns to Dad. "There's his snarky attitude." She scoffs. "I guess we know he's going to be okay."

As a multi-ton weight seems to squeeze against my skull, I wish I could be unconscious again. I look over and see two cards. One's a basic one of a flower bouquet that I know is from Rick and Jenny. I read their notes, put it aside, and look at the other one.

"Smile," it says on the front, alongside an illustrated smiley face. I gulp, thinking of Denise playing Nat King Cole at the Lantern. It's blank inside, although everyone's signed it in different colored pens.

Donna, in red.

> I know you're going to get through this. This isn't the way your story ends. I just know it isn't. Love you.

Frank, in blue.

You asshole. Get better.

Wally, in a yellow that's barely visible.

Love and light.

I'm about to cry, but I can't help but notice the one missing signature. "How long have I been out?"

"A day," Mom snaps. They're both still staring at me. "Don't you have anything to say for yourself?"

"Like what?" I snap back.

"I'm sorry for being snarky and rude to my parents who love me," Mom says, imitating me.

"Sorry," I mutter.

"Say it like you mean it," Mom says.

I'm trying to think of how to respond when Patty, rushing through the door, saves me. She's carrying a glass vase of daffodils as she and I lock eyes. She notices what I do—that there are no empty chairs.

"Patricia," Mom says.

She ignores them and rushes over to me. "Oh, God. Oh, God." She turns back to Mom and Dad. "When did he wake up?"

"A few minutes ago," Mom tells her.

Patty looks back to me, her eyes glassy. She puts the daffodils beside the cards. Mom and Dad glare at her as water splashes on the end table. "Have you called his nurse?" she asks them.

"In a minute," says Mom.

Patty leans down, blocking my parents from view. "I'm sorry, I just got off work, and the train here took forever and I had to get your flowers." She looks at Frank, Donna, and Wally's card and sniffles.

"I'm just glad you're here," I muster.

"Are you kidding? I would have come right here if I could have gotten coverage."

"You're not mad at me anymore?"

"Of course I'm still mad at you," she says. "But we're going to talk about it, right?"

As she strokes my hand and I do the same, I feel Mom and Dad's eyes on us.

"Hey, um..." She trails off, and then mouths the next. "Can you get rid of your parents?"

"Why?" I mouth back.

"Just for a minute," she says, giving me a "trust me" look.

I squeeze her hand and turn to Mom and Dad. "Can we have the room, please?"

"Why?" Mom demands.

"We need to have a private conversation," Patty says.

"We're his parents. Anything you have to say you can say in front of us," Mom says.

Patty rolls her eyes. She turns back to me and squeezes my hand even tighter. Her eyes are glassier still. "Tom, you have no idea..."

As tears stream down her cheeks, I feel my heart thumping. "What happened?"

Patty looks back at Mom and Dad and then leans in closer to me. "All of this time, I've been thinking about what to do," she whispers. "Because, I wanted... but I wasn't ready... and then Diane told me that she talked to you... then, I was ready. Then I didn't know..."

What on earth is she talking about?!

"But I'm so glad you're okay, because... I'm pregnant."

Mom gasps and Dad's face goes tight.

"What?" I say once I've processed.

"We're going to have a baby," she says, smiling now.

"Patty," I say, beaming. My headache has now evaporated.

"What do you think?" she asks, standing beside me.

"What do you want?" I finally manage.

"I want things to be different. They're going to have to be."

I pause, thinking of it myself. *I'm going to be a dad.* That's going to take a while to sink in. I always wanted kids, but I thought that was five years down the road at least. This is going to change everything. Maybe it's because I'm still not fully here, but none of that seems to matter. I know it's going to be okay as long as we're together. I take her hand and rub it. "Here's what we're going to do. We're going to have a long talk about everything because we're going to do what we need to do to give this child the best life they could ever dream of." As I talk, her smile grows, filling me with light.

"Sounds great to me," she finally says, her eyes filled with tears.

Mom and Dad stand up. "We're going to go find his nurse," Mom tells us. Of course, *now* they leave.

"By the way," Patty says once they're gone. "The hospital accountant? They quit. So the job is open again."

"I'll call Diane."

"You better," Patty says with a smile.

She stays with me for a little while longer until I fall back to sleep.

eighteen

I'M INSIDE THE LANTERN. At first, it seems like no one's there, even though I have a sense that it's being prepared for something. No, some*one*. And then I see him. The star of the show, sitting on the edge of the stage.

He's in jeans and a green-and-blue button-up. *My* green-and-blue button-up. How?

I think he'll see me, but he's too focused on his guitar. He's strumming.

I get a little further up when he sees me and stops.

"Don't stop," I say. "It's really nice."

Other than the fact that he's wearing my shirt, there's something familiar about him. "It's not ready yet," he mutters.

"What do you mean it's not ready? You're about to go on, aren't you?"

"Yeah," he says.

I take another step forward, and I get a good look at the musician. His hair is dark and wavy like mine. There's freckles on his cheeks and nose, and his eyes—Sinatra-blue like Patty's—are watery. He sniffles and wipes them away.

"Are you okay?" I ask.

"Sorry," he says. He scoots over and lets me sit. I get an even better look at him now. He's young, too. He can't be older than twenty. Twenty-one at the most. "There's someone I really wish was here tonight."

"Oh?" I tease. "Girl trouble?"

"For once, no," he says with a tired smile. "My dad."

"Your dad?" I repeat. "Why can't he be here?"

"He died," the musician says. "He was the one that got me into all of this."

"Oh? He must have been pretty cool," I say.

"He was the best person I've ever known," the musician whispers. He breaks down in tears now. I have the strongest urge to bring him into my arms, and I do.

"Hey," I say once he's relaxed. "Cool shirt. Where'd you get it?"

"It was my dad's."

When I open my eyes, it's early morning. I'm back in my hospital room. The clock at my bedside says it's 6:30. The effect of the dream lingers, but I can't quite piece it together. *Was the musician supposed to have been my son?* I shrug it off. It was just a dream. Besides, we don't even know if we're having a boy. Even if we did, how could I possibly know what he'd look like in twenty years?

Seeing Dad at my bedside immediately makes my headache return. He's reading a newspaper. He notices me and puts it aside. "They'll be in for your morning rounds in a minute. Your mother's opening up the shop."

"Got it."

"How did you sleep?" Dad asks.

"Fine."

"Got it. *Fine*," he repeats, mocking me.

I rub my temples. "Can you let me wake up a little bit first?"

"We need to talk about yesterday."

I notice the headline then: ROCKSTAR ARRESTED. I see a familiar streak of hair that I think I recognize even under the picture's black-and-white filter. Suddenly, a chill runs down by body. "What's the headline today?"

"Oh," he says, nonchalant as he pushes the paper down towards me. "Do you want to see it?"

I nod.

"In a minute," Dad says, rolling the paper up and holding it in one hand against his lap.

"Okay," I say.

"I thought we could discuss your plans and how it's going to fit in with your current lifestyle. I wouldn't say that house you're currently in is the best place to raise a child, is it?"

"No. Probably not."

I hold my hand out for the paper. Dad hesitates and then hands it to me.

My heart sinks. It's Denise. The dead stare of her mugshot makes my heart thump as I scan down to the article.

She'd been on the Sunset Strip the night before— completely naked. She'd told shocked witnesses that she just had to get to the Lantern Club in time for her show. One woman was so perturbed she gave her a dress she'd bought moments before from a nearby store. That did little as Denise continued to rant and rave about the street's missing Christmas tree—never mind that it was January. She ran into the middle of the street, twirling and singing. She was nearly hit by a car, rescued by a passerby, and pulled into an alleyway.

Thinking that the man who rescued her was her father, she kept telling him to go to hell. But he'd stayed with her nonetheless. Another woman came to assist, bringing Denise a cup of water from a nearby restaurant. She kept saying that she wasn't married and not to call her husband. Her feet were blistered. She must have walked from her house, ditching her clothes somewhere along the way.

I fold up the paper and put it aside, overwhelmed by a flash of Denise sobbing in the Lantern Club right before I broke her heart. *Where there any signs of what was coming? Anything that I'd missed?* Witnesses had all said her breath reeked of alcohol. But this felt like more than a night of going a little too far.

I can't help but feel at least a little responsible. I close my eyes and silently send her my best.

Dad and I just sit there in silence. In a desperate attempt to fill it, I gesture to the article. "You see this? Denise Peck?" As long as Rick keeps his promise, Dad will never know that I even met Denise, much less how far it went.

"Yep," Dad says. "She's lost. Everyone in that industry is, Tom."

Tom? What did I ever do to deserve this? "Not everyone," I say after a moment.

"Listen, I owe you an apology for our phone call when you were in LA," he says. "I know it must have been hard because you and the band worked so hard to get out there and even get seen for that audition. But all we've ever wanted is to make sure you're taken care of."

"I understand that," I say. I want to believe that he's genuine. I really, really do. "But it hurts me when you and Mom don't support the thing I love."

Dad laughs dryly. "I used to play ball, you know that?"

"Yeah." I can't think too much about playing catch in the summers when I was a kid, or how the only time I've seen my dad truly happy is on those fields. I especially can't think about the time he gifted me his old baseball cards and lit up as he shared fact after fact about every one of the players.

"We even made it as far as the state championships. It was my dream to go and play for the Yankees. But your mother and I got married right out of high school. I had to go to college to get a degree to provide for my family because we were about to have you."

"So I ruined your dreams?" I say with a scoff.

"No," Dad replies. "All I'm trying to tell you is that it's great to have them, but you won't just have yourself to look out for anymore."

"I know that," I say.

"You know you you're not going to be going to be able to get your record expunged this time, right?"

"I'm aware of that," I say. The only reason that happened with my first possession charges—which were later dropped anyways due to the "extenuating circumstances" of my mental distress—was because I was still under 21 and a new law had just passed.

"I talked to Brett Yates in our precinct and they're fairly certain you're just going to get a small fine as long as there weren't any other drugs in the house. Were there?"

"No," I lie.

"Then it should be fine."

I sigh, hating to think that I might have gotten the others in trouble. The thought didn't even cross my mind. I'm sure Wally would have acted fast in the time that it took for the ambulance to come get me. I can only hope.

After a long silence, I say, "to your earlier point, I'm going to give this child everything they could ever want."

"That's a nice thought, but—"

"I'm not finished, thank you." Dad blinks and his mouth forms a line as I continue. "I'm going to tell this child that they can be whatever they want to be. Whether that's music or baseball, or, heck, if they want to come work for you at the store, I'll support that too. Because it's going to be their life and no one else's. Do you understand *that?*"

"I do," Dad says. "What I've been trying to tell you, if you would just give me the chance, is that you can come back to the store."

"No." The truth of his apology is sinking in. I think he knows he's messed up and he and Mom are afraid they're not going to be a part of their grandchild's life. But I know that's going to be up to me. It's nice to take my power back.

"No?" Dad's face is white.

"I have a job lined up," I say.

"Do you really?"

"I do," I tell him. "Even if I didn't, I wouldn't come back. I never will."

Before Dad can respond, Lulu, my nurse, comes in for her morning rounds. He puts his mask on for her, asking how her morning's going so far and all that.

"It's good," Lulu says. "You know, still waking up. I think I need another cup of coffee."

"You've got to tell your boss to invest in those little machines in every room," he says jovially.

"That's a good idea," she replies. "Until then, can I bring you gentlemen some?"

"That would be lovely," he tells her with a smile.

"I'll be right back with two coffees," she says.

It's a small thing, but the fact that Dad spoke for me doesn't go unnoticed. I don't say anything because I would have agreed to a cup, but I think treating me like a child is a reflex for Mom and Dad. They just can't help themselves.

"Put whiskey in mine," Dad tells her. "I found out yesterday that I'm going to be a grandpa."

Lulu looks at me. I give her a nod.

"He got his girlfriend pregnant," Dad announces.

I try to think about how to respond to that when Lulu casts a smile at me. "Patty, right? Light-brown hair?"

I nod.

"Congratulations, Tom," Lulu says. "I think we're going to discharge you soon, but there's a psychiatrist that's going to come in and talk to you before that."

Ugh. Of course. This happened last time, too. There were a whole bunch of questions like if I felt hopeless or had thoughts of harming myself or others. I hadn't exactly answered honestly, but the truth was that I never actually wanted to die. I just wanted to stop feeling things for a while. And knowing that Patty is pregnant with our child—well, this changes everything, and for the better.

"I just need to pass that on," Lulu adds. "But it sounds like you have a lot to look forward to." After an awkward pause, she says, "I'll be back with two coffees. No whiskey."

She leaves, blushing slightly, and I turn to Dad. "Was that necessary?"

"Was what necessary?"

"The way you phrased it," I say.

"How did I phrase it?" Dad takes the newspaper back from my end table and starts to read it.

I roll my eyes. "Never mind. It's like trying to talk to the Cheshire Cat with you."

"That was uncalled for, Tom."

"It was uncalled for when you shared private information with my nurse," I retort.

"What private information? I'm just stating a fact."

I say nothing.

"By the way," Dad says, "have you thought about proposing?"

I scoff. *Of course I have.* But we need to resolve the Denise issue first, and Dad is never going to know about that. "Why would you even ask me that?"

"I'm just making sure."

"Well, it's the plan," I say. "It's not like I can get her a ring right now. I'm a little incapacitated."

The way Dad stares back at me with a raised eyebrow makes me more irritated by the second.

"What?"

"I think it should happen as soon as possible," he says.

"Why, so you don't have to carry the shame of your son having a kid out of wedlock?" From the way his face falls, I know that's the only reason.

"No, because your child should have stability," Dad asserts.

"Whatever."

Dad says nothing.

"By the way, when I do marry her it's because I want to spend the rest of my life with her. I want to wake up next to her every morning and be able to call her my wife."

"Then, I would prioritize that as soon as you get out," Dad says.

"That was the plan. What exactly is the conversation to be had here?"

"Might I remind you, Thomas, of the reason you're in this room?" Dad says, raising his voice. "Do you know who's going to be footing the bill?"

I don't respond.

"Your mother and I," he says sternly. "Whatever fine you get, though? That's going to be your responsibility."

"Sounds good," I say nonchalantly. "And, I didn't ask you to pay my hospital bills. So, I'm not sure what point you're trying to make."

Something hits me right then and there: This is the way he's always been. This is the way he always will be. Things could always change down the line—nothing's set in stone, after all—but as of right now I don't see any reason to believe that things are ever going to get better. Even when the kid is born, I'm sure he and Mom will find some way to criticize me and Patty for everything we're doing wrong. This is going to be the start of a new chapter for me, and I can't be around their energy anymore.

"We're trying to look after you."

"Well," I say curtly. "Stop. I'm an adult. And you need to trust me enough to make my own decisions."

"You're putting words in our mouths," Dad replies.

I lean back into my pillow. *We're going to keep going in circles to the end of time.*

Luckily, Lulu comes back with the coffees right then and there, preventing us from having to belabor the point any further.

Dad leaves not long after. I turn on the room's TV and find some reruns of *I Love Lucy* to help pass the time until Rick shows up.

I sigh and rub my temples as he walks in, remembering how we left things.

"What episode is this?" he asks.

"Not sure," I say. We watch for a minute before I realize it's the one where Lucy is pregnant. It's times like this where I think that if there is a God, he has an incredibly dry sense of humor.

I realize Rick's carrying a pastry bag. He takes one out and hands it to me. "I didn't know if you still liked Lou's, but I got you a chocolate croissant."

"Thanks," I say, accepting it and quickly taking a bite. It must have been ages since I've last had Lou's, but they're just as tasty as I remember. "I'm sorry about how I acted the last time we talked."

Rick waves me off. "Did my ears deceive me when I heard that I'm going to be an uncle?"

"No, they did not." I'm unable to stop my smile.

"Wow." Rick takes a bite into his croissant. "You and Patty are all good?"

"I think so," I say. "What did you tell Mom and Dad? About what happened?" I'm curious for the first time since I've woken up.

"As far as they're concerned, they have no idea you two

even had a fight," Rick says nonchalantly. "Honestly, Tom, the only reason it came up is that they thought she had an attitude at Christmas. I just said she's probably stressed with everything going on and told them not to worry about it."

"Thank you," I manage.

"I know I'm not much, but I do have my moments," Rick says.

We exchange a smile.

"Anyways," he continues. "Are you going to finally pop the question? Join us crusty, married folk? It's not such a bad time, I promise."

"We'll see," I say.

"Also, for what it's worth, I think what you do with the band and with music is awesome. I wish I was that passionate about something," he says.

I look at my brother's pleading, earnest stare and sigh.

He stays for a while and we end up flipping through the channels until we find *Goldfinger* just as the opening credits are rolling.

We'd both been so into James Bond as kids, so we don't need to say anything to mutually agree to keep it on. We watch until the end, when he leaves. Right after that, I fall back to sleep.

I WAKE with a start to find Patty sitting by my side. It's just past two in the afternoon. I look at her as she strokes my forehead.

"Hey," she says, her smile wide. "I'm off today."

I wrap her hand in mine and bring it up to my lips.

"You seem like you're doing good," she says as we continue to hold hands.

"I'm better now that you're here," I tell her. As we sit there, I think about the dream. I thought I'd resolved it back at the Chateau with Donna, but I need to tell someone. "So, I've been having this recurring dream about being at this concert waiting to see this musician. I had it again last night."

"Oh?" Patty asks curiously.

"A couple of months ago it was waiting to get inside the venue. Now, I've actually seen him and it's our son."

"Son? How do you know?"

"He was crying because I wasn't around anymore and he was wearing my shirt."

Patty nods along.

"He's a musician. He's famous, I guess. And the common thing is that everyone treats me like I'm a ghost."

"Oh. I guess I'm not sure what to say. How do the dreams make you feel?" She laughs wryly. "I know that's what Donna always says to think about."

I consider. "I think I'm sad because I'm proud of him but I know I'm going to have to go, even though I don't want to. You were in one. You were mad because I couldn't stay even though I told you that I could."

"Huh," Patty says. "That is strange."

Suddenly, it hits me. "You know, I think it's my brain telling me that things are going to have to change with this baby."

"I agree," she says.

"About Denise—" I start.

"What made that so hard was that she took all the responsibility. But I have to know... Tom... did you like her? Or at least, did any part of you want something to happen?"

"I was attracted to her," I admit. "And I think I wanted to help her since I couldn't help Jack."

Patty nods vaguely. "I heard about what happened."

"Yeah," I say, almost inaudibly.

"I saw that she had a huge fight with her husband? Like, she'd tried to leave him and he found her and brought her back, then she lost it. Who knows."

Oh. That's all news to me. I hope, if there's a silver lining to all of this, it's that Denise gets out of that marriage. She deserves so much better.

"I feel guilty," I admit.

"She should have known better, going after you," Patty says with a scoff, loosening her grasp on my hand. "Anyways, the second you dream of doing something like this again, it's over. Do you understand?"

I nod. "I'm committed to you, Patty. A thousand percent." The words are on the tip of my tongue. *In fact, I'm so committed to you I want to ask you if you'll marry me.* But I can't bring myself to push them out. Instead, I tell her, "I know you're going to have to give up drugs now, and I'm going to be right there with you."

"Tom, are you sure? That's a big thing to do."

"Look at me, Patty," I say.

As she does, I feel like I'm seeing her for the first time all over again.

"I almost died. And past that, if I hadn't been lucky with my close calls I'd be in jail. I don't want it to happen again or for our kid to grow up without a father. We've got to be there for him—or her—completely."

She nods. "I can talk to Gracie. She knows some good recovery programs. I think some of her friends have been through it. Just to help keep us in check."

"Sounds great to me," I say with a smile.

Patty just smiles.

The lull envelops the room.

Now, you coward.

Now's your chance.

"Patty," I start, taking her hand again.

"Yeah?"

"I love you."

"I love you, too," she says.

"I've been thinking a lot about this, and you know, it's been a bug in my ear even before all of this..."

"Mm-hmm..." she says.

"When I was gone, when you were gone, the thing I couldn't stand the most was not waking up next to you."

Patty leans in closer. "Say more."

"I always want to wake up next to you."

She rubs my hand. "I'm listening."

"Would you ever want to... be my wife?"

"Are you asking me to marry you, Thomas Hargrove?" Patty says. Somehow, my full name is okay when she says it. Her smile fills me with light.

"If that's what you want, Patty-cake."

"Are you kidding?"

"I would never," I tell her, bringing her hand to my lips and kissing it.

"Then do it right," she says with a smile and a sniffle.

"Well," I say. "I can't exactly get down on one knee or get

you a ring right now, but, Patricia Josephine Reilly, will you marry me?"

She nods. "Yes." Her kiss is hesitant at first, and it's quick, but it's all I need to know that everything's going to be okay.

THAT AFTERNOON, the psychiatrist, an older woman who reminds me of a librarian with her white hair in a beehive, slouch and glasses tied around her neck with a chain, comes to pay me a visit. I remember all of these questions, but this time, I answerer them honestly.

Do I never, rarely, sometimes, often or always feel sad or hopeless about the future?

A week ago, the answer would have been often, but now, it's sometimes.

What about excessive feelings of guilt?

Often.

Low self-esteem?

Always.

Loss of pleasure in daily activities?

"I don't have pleasure in anything except my friends, my girlfriend—fiancée, as of today, sorry—and music," I tell the psychiatrist.

She smiles tiredly. "You sound just like my son. We all have to follow the things that make us happy."

After her questions are finally done, the psychiatrist writes things down for what seems like forever.

"I'm diagnosing you with clinical depression. It's very common. Some of my colleagues are calling it Major Depressive Disorder, but it's the same thing. It's up to you to decide if you want to speak to someone in the future, but I'll advise that you're okay to be discharged." She hands me a paper. It's a referral for a psychiatrist in town. "Congratulations on your engagement."

I have depression. Huh. I feel like that's going to explain a lot. I look at the paper again. Maybe doing this won't be such a bad thing.

THE NEXT DAY—THE day I get discharged—Frank, Donna, and Wally meet me in my room with a breakfast of bagels and cream cheese.

"Oh my goodness," Donna keeps saying over and over. "I can't believe you guys are going to be parents! And getting married, too. I mean, I can. I don't think there was any doubt in my mind."

"I'm still processing that," I tell them. "Plus the fact that I'm clinically depressed and have a referral for a shrink." Rick brought me some literature from the library on the DSM-II last night, and it sure sounded like me.

"In your sessions, only say nice things about us," Donna says.

"I don't think that it works like that," Wally cuts in.

Donna smirks. "I'm sure I'm depressed, too, anxious and who knows what else. We can all be freaks together."

"You guys. I have an idea," Frank announces. "What if we were all hermits instead?"

There's a long, unmistakable beat of silence as we all suppress laughs.

Wally imitates the chirping of crickets, and all of us lose it.

"Anyways," I say once we pull ourselves together. "About the drugs. Bad news is, the possession thing is going to be on my record. I'll be able to pay the fine now with the new job. I'll do community service or whatever else they need me to do. I'm happy to help any of you…"

I notice the others are already shaking their head and trail off.

"It's fine," Donna says. "Wally got rid of everything before they came."

I look at Wally. "Yeah, man. All down the toilet."

I picture the scene in my head. Wally, finding me, calling the cops, and then panicking once he knew our stashes would spell trouble.

"I think the cop was suspicious but I don't think he cared enough to ask questions," Wally continues.

"I'm so sorry," I tell them all. "Things are going to be different now. This time, I mean it."

"I know," is all Donna says.

"I don't know the first thing about being a father," I admit. "I'm going to get better for their sake. For Patty's. I have to."

"And we'll be right there with you until we die," Donna says.

"Unless I die first," I tease. "I'm not outliving any of you. That's not happening."

"You can't. I thought we stablished that I'm dying first," Wally says.

I smirk. This is a bit from I want to say, driving up to Springfield, Massachusetts for the second Dead show, when we were still getting to know each other. I have no clue how we got on the subject in the first place, but it made me think, as I do now, about how things have always been black after around fifty. But I keep those thoughts to myself, especially as Donna rolls her eyes.

"Come on, guys," she scolds. "No one's dying." Then, she turns to me. "We love you, Tom."

"Love you too," I reply with a smile.

nineteen

AFTER CINDY and I broke up, I thought my life was over. I'd spent four years sleepwalking through my accounting classes at Newark Community College and ended up a carless, jobless, strung-out loser forced to come groveling to my parents.

I never thought I'd get another chance. But I did, on that scorching-hot summer day in 1974 when Rick and I were supposed to go see the Grateful Dead. Him bailing and leaving me forced to hitch a ride would change my life forever. The driver could only take me as far as a rest stop outside of New Haven. That was okay—I'd find someone to take me the rest of the way. I was sure of it. I was an anxious twenty-two year old on that summer day, sitting and baking in the heat on the side of the highway. Dozens of cars zipped right by me. One person who stopped claimed they were going too far out of the way for it to makes sense.

I had needed to pee, so I walked down the side of the narrow road, telling myself I would do what I needed to do and circle around the lot before I hitched back to Newark and forgot about the whole thing. I exited the main building and had eyed a vending machine, figuring I'd use some of my spare change to treat myself to a Sprite.

I'd just paid when I saw the VW bus. Then I saw Donna and Frank get out, looking over a map. She was still Donna Byrne then, and the unpainted bus was its natural yellow.

"We're doing great on time," Frank said to her. "By the way, I packed the grass."

"Yay," she said, giving him a peck on the lips.

"We'll have to bum beers off someone, though," Frank said.

"It's cool," Donna replied.

Wherever these people were going, I figured they'd at least be good company. I grabbed my soda from the machine and turned towards them. "Hey," I called, getting their attention. "You got room for one more?"

"Where are you going?" Donna said with a smile.

"Providence," I said.

Donna's eyes widened. "No way. We're going to Providence."

"What for?" I asked.

"The Dead," Frank said.

"Me too."

Donna lit up. "Come on in."

Wally came out of the van too, and we all introduced ourselves.

"Yeah, it's my first time so I don't really know what to expect," I told them.

Donna squealed. "You found the right van, Tom."

"I hope so."

From the first moments in the car, it felt like I'd known them my whole life. Wally drove that day. Frank was in front, and I was with Donna in the back.

"Tom, what's your favorite Dead song?" she asked me.

"Ooh... maybe 'Ship of Fools' or 'Friend of the Devil.' But it's so hard to pick."

"There truly is no wrong answer," she said. "You know, believe it or not, I saw them in Haight-Ashbury before they were famous."

"She's only going to rub that in your face every chance she gets," Frank told me with a smile.

I smiled back, only realizing later on that it was my first real smile in a long, long time.

"Yeah, I've played keys all my life," Donna told me. "These guys... they're just fucking life changing. After Pigpen died... it just made me be like... let's go for it."

"Sorry, some context here," Frank said. "We're all musicians."

"Pigpen was my favorite," Donna said. "I'm sad you don't get to see him, but it's going to be an amazing show."

Pigpen. Ron McKernan. That was his real name. I remember hearing about his death, two months after Jack's. Dad had used it to try and impart some lesson about how pursuing music only ever led to a life of misery. But that was the year I'd listened to everything they'd ever recorded and became a convert. "Yeah, I'm a musician too," I said. "My partner... he died. He was the one that introduced me."

"I'm sorry," Donna said. "He'll be here watching over us."

"Just like Pigpen," Wally said from the driver's seat. He turned up the radio. "Tom, what do you play?"

"Bass," I said.

Donna gasped, looked over at Frank and Wally, and then back at me. "No way."

"Yes way."

"We're trying to start a band. We have been for a while, but we've always been missing a bassist," she said. "Do you really play bass?"

"Yes, I really do," I told her with a laugh.

"Okay, we just met, so we're not going to jump into anything, but let us take you home tonight. Are you in New Haven?" she asked.

"No. Newark," I said.

Donna's mouth fell open. "Stop. We live in Newark."

It all seemed divinely guided, if there ever was such a thing.

I met Patty there, too, at that concert. We'd found a spot to camp out. She was right there, beside us, with Diane and Gracie. They were drinking—what was it? Miller High Life, I think.

Gracie had a camera over her neck and her arm around Diane. She turned her camera towards her girlfriend and snapped a picture. As she did, Patty and I locked eyes and gestured to their cooler. "You want one?"

I turned back to my new friends, and they gave me their silent permission to go for it.

"Hi, I'm Patty," she said. "My sister and I are from Long Island. But we live in Manhattan now."

"I'm Tom from Newark," I replied, shaking her hand. "Pleasure." She introduced me to Diane and Gracie and we all chatted a little. I thought that Patty from Long Island was the most beautiful woman I'd ever seen. Her blue eyes were the first thing I noticed. I couldn't stop looking at them, how they sparkled in the sun, and how cute her freckles were.

I know I made her nervous because she told me that in the time that followed. But then she said, "have you been to one of these before?"

I shook my head and spit out what was in my head. "The color of your eyes... reminds me of Frank Sinatra."

Patty blushed and looked back at Diane and Gracie. "Well, that's a first. I don't sing like Frank Sinatra, but thank you."

"I don't either," I told her. "I stick to guitar. Bass."

"I love music. I wish I could do it, but I'll be a proud appreciator," Patty said.

"What do you love about it?" I asked.

"It brings people together," she said. She scanned the crowd that surrounded us. "Just look at this. This is my third time and it never won't be amazing."

"What do you love about the Dead?" I asked her.

"It shouldn't work, but it does," she said.

She'd just vocalized something I'd been struggling to put into words for months.

"Do you want to go on a walk with me, Patty?" I asked before I had a chance to overthink it. I didn't know what I was expecting, but I knew I wanted to keep talking to her.

Then, shortly before we had to start heading in, I got scared and ran away.

Frank was disappointed with me, but I told him, "Hey, maybe I'll see her again at the next one."

The show itself was everything I wanted it to be and more.

They dropped me off at the apartment I was renting at the crack of dawn with plans to meet up for their show in Springfield, Massachusetts the following week. Then, I'd see if I was still interested in being a part of their band.

FAST FORWARD A WEEK to Springfield and concert two. My new friends and I had been relaxing outside the venue for a while when I heard, "Hey, Tom from Newark."

Patty, again. I stood up and faced her, ignoring the sly smiles from my new friends. "Hey again!"

"It's just me and Diane today," she said.

"Do you want to meet my friends?" I asked.

"Sure." I scooted over to make a place for her, she sat down, and I introduced her to the group.

We were having a great time, laughing, bonding, being in the moment. Sitting beside her was intoxicating enough, but as soon as we tripped, the feeling only intensified. The acid was just starting to take hold when Diane passed by our picnic blanket.

"There you are," she told Patty. She didn't say a word to me, but I knew she recognized me from before. "Do you want to stay with them? You can find me later."

"I'll come with you," Patty said, standing up and darting away, managing a wave goodbye in my direction.

Everyone was looking at me. "What?"

"*Run after her!*" Donna exclaimed. "Her face was bright red. You guys are so into each other. It's obvious."

"Uh, maybe not," I said. "You guys, she's with her sister."

"And you're bright red, too, oh my gosh!" she squealed.

"Alright, Tom," Frank said. "If you see this girl again, you have no excuse for not asking her out."

It would be a long month until the Dead came to Jersey

City. We passed it by jamming once a week. We played well together, and I'd forgotten how good it felt to be playing music again. We were still deciding on a name for the band on a beautiful August night, my third show.

There she was, outside the venue. I sat with her and Diane that night. Gracie and I switched tickets to make it happen.

After the show, once we reconvened, I found out Gracie had become fast friends with the others.

"We're stealing her," Frank informed Diane.

"You can have her for a million dollars," Diane teased as Gracie went to rejoin her.

As we all discussed how close we were to home, and thus didn't have hours-long drives ahead, Diane and Gracie mentioned wanting to check out a lesbian bar they knew was close by. They knew it wouldn't really be Patty's scene and didn't want her to be stuck with them or to have to go back alone.

I knew that was my in. "Patty, if you want, I can ride into the city with you. We can find some food if you're hungry? My treat."

Patty's ear-to-ear grin was something I'd never forget. "Alright."

"Be safe, Pats," Diane said. Then, she turned to me. "By the way Tom, I'm a black belt in karate."

We exchanged waves as she and Gracie walked off into the night, passing Frank, Donna, and Wally as we moseyed in the direction of the station.

"I won't need a ride tonight, guys," I said.

"No problem," Donna said, smiling. "Next week? Same Bat-time, same Bat-channel?"

I saluted.

"What's happening next week?" Patty asked.

"Jamming. We're going to make this band official soon, just trying to decide on a name."

"Any contenders?"

"Well, Donna keeps pitching the Hermit Crabs. Because they hide in their shells and she relates to that or something. But I don't want to be a crab."

Patty laughed. "What about just The Hermits?"

That's it. I knew it. She didn't even have to explain. "I'll pitch it to them."

That night, we ate pizza, walked around the streets of Manhattan, and ended up in a park, where we shared our first kiss. That was August 6th, 1974.

On April 19th, 1978, she became my wife.

Diane's condition would deteriorate not long after, but that day, she was well enough to come, even if it was in a wheelchair. At the reception, we leaned down to hug her as Gracie stood close.

Diane handed Patty an envelope. She was losing the ability to speak. Her voice was crackly and hoarse, but we understood. "What's left from Mom and Dad."

We opened the envelope. It was a check for $500.

A week later, we found out we were having a boy.

The name was tough to figure out. We'd both quickly agreed on Kelsey for a girl but had no ideas for boys. We decided on Franklin—after Frank—for his middle name pretty early on. For a while it didn't seem like we'd ever agree on a first. I vetoed Calvin. She vetoed Timothy. I vetoed Ken. She vetoed Christopher.

"What's wrong with Christopher?" I said.

"I want him to have a name you don't hear every day," she

said. "What about Cole?"

"Cole?"

"It's musical," she said. "Just like his dad. Cole Porter, Nat King Cole..."

"Cole Hargrove," I said. "I like the sound of that."

In July, we moved out of the Newark house that had given us so many memories and into the extra bedroom of Diane and Gracie's apartment in Queens. It wasn't ideal. While there was a third bedroom, Gracie used it as her home photography studio, so when Cole was born, he'd have to be in with us. But that was okay, for now.

"Gracie could really use the help," Patty told me. "She acts like she can't be bothered by anything but I'll feel better if we're there. Especially once Diane goes to hospice, you know?"

I'd started seeing Dr. Cotter, the psychiatrist on my referral, twice a month once I got out of the hospital. He was a guiding force through our journey towards sobriety and parenthood. I was sad to leave him behind, but he was able to refer me to a new doctor in the city.

"I figure you guys can be here until Diane goes or you two get tired of us," Gracie said once we officially moved in.

"Gracie, it's perfect," I said.

"Good," she said with a sniffle. "Welcome to New York."

We didn't leave Newark before making one last stop at the car dealership, though. An Oldsmobile Cutlass was there. Not the same one, of course. This was a 1971 model, and bright red, which I liked even more then the black. $3,200. Between what I'd managed to save at the new job and Diane's generous gift, I was able to put a downpayment on it. The salesman—the same one who'd helped us on that summer day the year before—gave us another $200 off the sticker price because, in his words, "I like you folks."

The first time I got into the driver's seat is something I'll always treasure.

I kissed Patty deeply as she slid into the passenger's side.

Finally.

I'M THINKING about all of this—about how everything seemed to lead to this moment—the first time I hold my son in my arms.

Cole Franklin Hargrove is born on September 15th, 1978, and everything changes that day. He'd thankfully inherited his mother's blue eyes and freckles.

"It's a good thing he takes after you," I say.

"He's going to have your hair," Patty says. "I know it."

"I'll allow it," I reply with a smirk. The hairs on my skin rise I think about the vision of the musician from my dreams. But I shrug it off. I don't need dreams anymore, not when everything I've ever wanted is right in front of me.

Cole has a great big smile on his face when Patty hands him to me.

"Cole," I say. "Welcome to earth, bud. Enjoy the ride."

Cole just cries.

The next day, Rick and Jenny show up. Patty holds Cole in her arms when they come into the room. It's still been radio silence from Mom and Dad.

"How does it feel?" Rick says, tapping my shoulder.

"Still sinking in," I say.

Once they both meet their nephew, Jenny holds him first. I turn to Rick.

"What's their excuse now?"

"They're coming tomorrow," Rick says. "They're busy at the store."

I nod. *Typical.* "They could at least pretend to care."

Rick sighs. "Not now, Tom. Jesus Christ."

"Why not? You know they're bitter it wasn't you first."

Rick says nothing and looks over to Jenny. She looks back at him, and hands Cole to Rick.

"He's so expressive already," she tells me.

"Yeah, I..." All I can do is grin. "We'll see."

Cole starts to cry again, and Rick gives him back to Patty. Then, he sits, takes Jenny's hand, and they both face me.

"Anyways..." Jenny starts "we haven't wanted to... take away from you guys, but"—she's blushing as she rubs her stomach—"soon, Cole's going to have a cousin to play with."

"Rick! Jenny!" Patty exclaims. "Congratulations!" She's started to calm Cole down, but he starts crying again. "You hear that?" she asks him. "Soon you're not going to be the only cute baby around."

I watch with a smile as Patty kisses Cole's forehead. Then, I turn back to my brother and sister-in-law. "Everything's changing, isn't it?"

"It sure is," Rick says with a grin.

As PROMISED, Mom and Dad come the next day.

"How's everything at the hospital?" Dad asks me as Mom holds Cole, referring to my job.

"Fine," I reply.

"Just fine?"

"Yeah," I say. "It's actually going pretty well."

"Good," Dad says. "We're proud of you, son."

I smirk as Mom gives Cole to Dad. "Rick told me his news, too."

"It feels like it was just yesterday we were putting diapers on you both," Mom says wistfully. She turns to Patty. "When do all of you get out of here?"

"Hopefully tomorrow," she says. "There's going to be a lot to do while we figure out what life looks like with this guy."

"I would hope that means making plenty of time to visit his grandparents," Dad says. He hands Cole back to me now.

After I secure him in my arms, I let Dad's comment sink in. I wasn't going to say anything, not now. But I can't hold back. "I've been thinking about this a lot. And this doesn't change anything about the last year... the last five, or really, my whole life depending on how far back you want to go. I put a river between us for a reason. If you ever come to our side, I don't want to know about it. I don't want you two to call us at all. I want you to let us be, and let us raise our son. Because I've finally realized something. I'm not a child—"

"Thomas," Dad starts. "No one's saying—"

"Let me finish!" Cole starts crying again, and I give him back to Patty. Once he settles down, I continue. "You two have always made me feel like I'm never enough. Why? Because I want to make music and bring joy into other people's lives? Because I happened to meet people I love that share that dream? Because we tried?"

I watch as their faces fall.

"If you thought because of this that we were giving up, you're wrong. I'm going to be a part of The Hermits until I die, okay?"

They still have nothing to say.

"When you do see your grandson, it will be on our terms, and our terms only. Do you understand?"

In response. Dad stands up. Mom follows him as they gather their things, and she takes his hand. "Best of luck to you," he says.

They leave without another word.

OUR JOY IS SOON TAINTED by the fact that Diane doesn't have much time left. In the days before, she'd been placed in hospice. Once Patty is discharged from the hospital, we go to visit her.

"This is Cole," Patty tells her sister. To him, she says, "Your aunt Diane."

Cole just cries as Patty rocks him back and forth.

She can't move. She can't speak. But I know, from the look in her eyes, that she's engaged with us. That she knows.

She dies on May 30th, 1979, surrounded by me, Patty, Gracie, and Cole.

Later that night, after Cole's in bed, we all sit around the coffee table with wine.

"What are we going to do about this place?" Gracie asks. "I mean, you guys need the space more than me."

"We can't afford it without you," I say.

"Cole's going to need a room of his own eventually, isn't he?" Gracie says.

"We can set up a bed in the studio, can't we?" Patty asks.

"Sure," Gracie replies. "For now. I would move out, but it's hard to find the motivation for anything."

"Don't worry about that," Patty reassures her. "It was your place first. We'll just take things one day at a time."

"Hey," she says. "I was cleaning stuff out and I found some film from our '74 shows. I can get the projector going if you guys want to watch?"

"Of course," I say. "If that's what you want to do."

"Yeah, I actually wanted to show Diane but I could just never find the reel for whatever goddamn reason. And today, finally I found it. You want to know where it was?"

"Where?" I ask.

"It somehow had gotten wedged behind one of my file cabinets. All that time... it might be a little damaged, but I have video and slides. I haven't watched so I don't know what's on there but... please, I don't want to do this alone."

We agree without hesitation.

The second everything's set up and we're ready to watch, Cole starts crying.

"Of course," Patty says with a sigh. "I'll get him."

"You two are going to have to get used to this," Gracie mutters with the slightest of smiles.

Once she exits down the hallway, Gracie stares at me for a long moment. "Whoever would have thought," she whispers.

"What?" I ask.

She's still smiling. "Never mind."

It must be a few minutes of us just sitting there, listening to Patty. She's singing him something. It's so familiar...

I get up and go down the hall to our room, careful as I open the door. It's old, beautiful... "I Bring You A Song." It's working.

"You should sing to him more," I whisper. "What's it from?"

She smiles at me. "*Bambi*," Patty whispers back. "It was

our favorite, both me and Diane... It's been in my head all freaking day."

"I remember," I say, squeezing her shoulder.

"Hey, look, it's Daddy," Patty tells Cole.

"Mama's singing you a song," I tell him. "You like that?"

Cole opens his droopy eyes, reaches his chubby little hand towards me, and smiles.

After a moment, Patty carefully puts him back in his crib.

As soon as I open the door, he starts crying again.

Patty groans. "Sweetie, what do you want?"

He stops once she's scooped him back up in her arms.

"He wants us," I say, offering to take him. Once I do, I look at him again. "You want to see old videos of Mama and Dada?"

His peaceful look is the answer we need.

GRACIE'S SITTING PATIENTLY in the living room. She sees Cole and gives us an empathetic look. "He wanted to watch," I explain as we sit down on the couch.

"Of course, he is more than welcome," she says, giving him a goofy look, which makes him smile.

My eyes notice the screen now. It's a still of a bright summer day in Providence, Rhode Island. The focus is on a man in a tie-dye shirt and woman in a blue-and-red floral blouse. Me, Patty. The day we met. I inhale.

That day feels like so long ago, like it only exists in my memory.

Gracie's blushing as she starts the projector. A second later, I know why.

"Look at that, they're back," Gracie narrates from within the tape. "How long were they on that walk?"

"About twenty-five minutes," Diane says.

Oh, gosh... her voice...

"I'm sure they had a great time circling the grounds," Gracie, on video, teases. She turns the camera on Diane. She's glowing, smiling, wearing a long white dress, her hair stick straight as she lounges on a red-checkered picnic blanket, one I remember well. I'd almost forgotten what she *looked* like—healthy, anyway. "What do we think of Mr. Tom from Newark?"

"He's pretty cute," Diane says playfully.

Gracie pauses the projector. Her face is bright red. Patty's and mine both are, too.

"Oh my goodness," Gracie says. "I completely forgot about that."

"You filmed us?" Patty asks.

"We..." She laughs now. "I was trying to find something to focus on and suddenly I saw you two."

"Keep playing," I say.

Gracie obliges. The video turns back to us. We're a few steps closer now. We talk to a man with his back to us. The angle blocks out most details, but I remember it well. The guy had a slouch and these big glasses with thick frames. He wanted to interview us for his radio show.

I'd forgot what he'd asked—something insinuating Patty and I were a couple, and that's when I dipped. The video hasn't gotten to that part yet.

"Well look at that, your sister's a celebrity," Gracie says on video.

I notice Cole's watching intently. *There it is.* I dart off, probably to circle the place one more time. Patty's rejoined Diane and Gracie on the picnic blanket. She's smiling.

"Have fun?" Diane says.

"Shut up," Patty whispers.

"See," I whisper to Cole. "That's Mama and Dada the day they first met. It was at a concert for the Grateful Dead." His eyes are laser focused on the projector screen, but I keep on talking. "And I met your Godpapa Frank, and your Godmama Donna and your other Godpapa Wally that day, too. And it all led to you."

epilogue

IT'S a crisp fall day in Brooklyn, in Prospect Park. My son—
unbelievably—just turned two years old. Gracie moved out of
the apartment and back to Maine earlier in the year, leaving the
place to us. She left us most of the pictures and photos from
the Dead concerts. I'll show them to Cole one day, when he's
old enough.

Right after Gracie left, Patty and I watched the interview
she'd done of us in Englishtown. We'd been so full of hope that
day. I can see it in our eyes and the way we talk. We thought
stardom would solve all of our problems then.

Watching the footage, I realize something else.

I think these days are behind me. Traveling, waiting for
hours on end, getting high as a kite to pass the time—it doesn't
have the same appeal. And that's okay. Once a Deadhead,
always a Deadhead.

Besides, The Hermits had never really stopped going out
for gigs. Obviously, it all took a backseat to raising Cole. But
now that he's starting to walk and talk, the others finally joined

us in New York so we could start taking things more seriously again.

Donna, Frank, and Wally have all been obsessed with their godson since the day he was born. It's Frank who insisted he and Patty come to watch the photoshoot. We all pooled money to hire the photographer, but no one needs to know that. Anyone who's thinking of hiring us just needs to know we're important enough to get our picture taken.

The rest of the band is already set up amongst the autumn foliage, but my bass still sits underneath the bench. Cole has been squirming all over the place and containing him today has been a task both Patty and I can barely handle. He learned to walk the previous summer, and now he can't get enough of it. Patty's secured him on his lap—for now—as I approach.

"Dada!" Cole exclaims. He tries to stand as I reach underneath for the case.

"Not right now, sweetie, okay," Patty whispers, kissing his forehead. She secures him in her arms once again, and he's a captive audience as I unpack my bass.

Later, Rick and Jenny are coming for a visit and they're bringing Dawn. My niece is fourteen months old and she's the only one that matches Cole in energy. The first time they met, they both tried to peacock the other for the attention of the four of us. Hopefully, he'll get out some of his rambunctiousness with Dawn. I wonder if Rick will try to bring up reconciling with Mom and Dad again. I hope not.

I saw a lot of them when Dawn was born. At first, there was a lot of passive-aggressive blame for me breaking up the family and depriving them of a relationship with their grandson. After that they seemed to mellow out, but I can't help but feel it's a trick to get me to start talking to them again. It's amazing not having to walk on eggshells all the time has done for my peace. I've called them on holidays, and we've sent cards for the past two years. For now, that's all I'm willing to do.

Until then—

"This is a bass guitar," I explain to Cole. I strum it in a playful motion. "You play the strings—"

Cole beams as if he's the happiest kid in the entire world.

"And out comes... music!"

Cole smiles and reaches his hand forward, but Patty pulls it back.

"Are you corrupting your son, Tom?" Frank's voice calls.

Before I can answer, he scoots next to Patty and Cole on the bench. His guitar still hangs over his body by its strap.

In response, Cole reaches his hand forward. He just barely plucks one of the strings before Patty pulls his hand back.

"Sweetie, what did we say about touching things that aren't yours?" Patty says scoldingly.

Frank isn't bothered by it in the slightest. Instead, he looks at me, smiling. "You see that, Tom?"

"My son is sticking his hands where they don't belong?" I say with a smirk.

"No," Frank replies, smiling wider. "It's fate."

"What is?"

"He's going to be a musician," Frank says. "I know it."

I laugh. "Only if he wants to."

"I have a feeling about these things." He stands up and pats me on the shoulder. "Come on. I think everyone's getting anxious."

I see Donna, Wally, and the photographer further down, looking in our direction. "I'll be right there."

"You got it." As Frank continues on ahead, I sit on the bench, next to my wife and son.

I kiss her on the lips, and then I kiss his forehead.

If only time could move in slow motion. I never thought it could be like this even a few years before.

I want to treasure not just every second, but every single solitary moment with my family. This was what I was waiting for all along. There's nothing else on earth I need.

acknowledgments

Writing this book challenged me in more ways than one, and I'm grateful to those who helped me bring it to fruition.

First and foremost, thanks to Jake Brennan, as I've been fascinated by the Grateful Dead ever since you first hired me to research them. Considering that job led to *About A Girl*, it seems apt that this story now leads into the music romance of *All Our Yesterdays*.

Connor Fineran and Kyle McCue for reading drafts of the book and offering thoughtful feedback. L. Theodoora for doing the same, and for being one of this series' biggest champions. Mike Hurst—thank you for adding a thoughtful Deadhead's eye to this story.

Mom and Dad, for helping me pick out Rick and Cindy's cars. Madi Taylor, for always being around to brainstorm and toss ideas.

The Velvet Records books are about people who create art in search of something greater than themselves, and in the words of Joan Didion, why we tell ourselves stories in order to live. With *Deadheads*, I especially aimed to paint a different side of the artistic struggle, one that has inherent meaning no matter where it leads. However it resonated, thank you to my readers for giving this story your precious, limited time.

velvet records

Deadheads is only the start of the world of Velvet Records. The story picks up in the 90s—keep reading for a sneak peak at *All Our Yesterdays*.

all our yesterdays

one

It all started on the night of my high school graduation, back in 1999, when my best friend Maura shoved a camcorder towards my face. Our class of forty-seven milled about in the orchestra room, waiting for the approaching announcement that it was time to line up and head in. My dad had just left for the auditorium, ready to conduct the underclassmen who'd play us through the night.

"Marcy Lewis, you're graduating! Have a comment?"

I blurted out the first thing to come to mind. "Happy Y2K!"

"What's the thing you're proudest of?" she asked. She took a step back to get a better shot, bumping into Georgia Hale.

"*Pay attention*," Georgia snipped. She walked off to find her friends.

Maura rolled her eyes, pausing the video.

"Never have to see her again," I said as soon as she was out of earshot.

"Good riddance," Maura said under her breath. She focused the camera on me once more. "Let's go from where we left off." She restarted filming, mimicking the motion of a slate with her thumb and index finger.

"All four years?" I clarified.

"All four years," she confirmed. "Pick one."

"Playing Nora in *A Doll's House*." I rarely had the time to do school plays, but the past spring, I had. Not only was it a special show, but there was a part of me that had a feeling it would be my swan song to theater, at least for a while.

"Perfect." Maura noticed her ex, Jack. She trailed after him with her camcorder in hand, asking him the same question. "What's the thing you're proudest of?"

As I watched them, my smile faded. While the two of them had broken up amicably after nearly two years together, I knew they still deeply cared for one another. It was hard not to envy the bond they'd shared.

I'd never had a boyfriend or even been on a date. I knew I wasn't ugly; the celebrity comparison I most often got was Winona Ryder. Even if my hair was a shade lighter, it had always stuck. But it was Maura, with her dark wavy hair, wide blue eyes, and soft features, that got heads to turn whenever we were together.

I scanned the room. My classmates wore royal blue caps and gowns, laughing, talking, taking pictures. I'd spent years imagining this day, and now it was here. It was then that I realized I hadn't thought about what came next. I hadn't committed to college. I decided to stay with my parents in our little town and find a job instead. When we'd talked through my plans, they'd made it very clear that I had a year of their support. By June 2000, they expected me to have a job, be enrolled in college, or both, and I would have to support myself.

My eighteenth birthday was in two days, and the day after it, my sister Eileen and I would be on our way to New York City. The previous year, at Christmas, our parents had gifted us money to book the trip, all expenses paid. Their reason was that, since we were both graduating, me from high school and her from college, it would be the perfect opportunity to do something on our own. New York had always fascinated the both of us. Eileen loved the fashion and culture. I was obsessed with Broadway and wanted to check out the real settings of movies I loved like *When Harry Met Sally* and *Cruel Intentions.*

My thoughts suddenly drifted to twelve students in Colorado who had been at the forefront of the country's mind for the previous six weeks, students who would not be graduating, not this year, not ever. The news coverage of the Columbine High School shooting and learning about the victims had become a morbid obsession for me. It seemed to especially stick with our senior class because we were in the same grade as the shooters. Columbine's student body had gone to school expecting April 20th to be just another day. How could they ever have known? How could life be so fragile?

April 21st was a solemn day at school. Most lesson plans were forgotten and replaced with open discussions where we shared our feelings about what happened.

Amidst finals, I'd had to pull away from the news and thoughts of Columbine, but standing in the orchestra room in my cap and gown, it all came back. A thought spun through my head. *Why do I get to graduate, and they don't?*

It would go unanswered. I realized I'd spaced out again when I noticed Maura standing beside me. She must have put her camera away. "You okay?" she asked.

"Yeah," I said.

"Hey!" she squealed. "We made it!"

"We sure did."

We hugged. Tears of joy welled in both of our eyes.

"Sorry about the interview stuff, by the way," she said. "I just thought it could be for my kids one day, or the twenty-five-year reunion."

"You never have to apologize, you know," I said with a smile. "I can't wait to brag to people about how I used to know Maura Woodson."

Maura pursed her lips, blushing. From the time we were young, she'd always had a camera in her hand, in a constant search for ways she could capture moments in time.

"How's packing going?" I asked after a beat. By the time Eileen and I got back from New York, Maura would be in Tallahassee. She'd been accepted to Florida State University's film school for the start of their summer semester.

Maura laughed. "Marcy, I don't want to think about packing right now! We're freaking graduating!" When I blushed, she added, "It's fine. I just want to be there."

"It's not going to be the same without you here," I said. I was happy for her, happy for her opportunity, but I would still selfishly miss her.

"I know."

"Are we still doing breakfast on my birthday?" I asked.

"I think—" she started.

We were shortly interrupted by the announcement that it was time to line up.

"See you on the other side," Maura said. We exchanged a quick wave as she went to find her place with the other Ws.

Shortly after that, we heard the unmistakable bellow of "Pomp and Circumstance." My heart immediately started pounding.

This was all really happening.

It was hard not to get emotional as we filed in. I thought about how boring this would be without the music. We'd just be walking in. But "Pomp and Circumstance" made it dramatic, important.

I spotted my mom and Eileen, but her boyfriend, Dan, was missing. He was supposed to have one of my tickets. Most of our extended family had come up for Eileen's graduation and our combined party with the intent to celebrate the both of us. My father was conducting the orchestra and band that would play us through the night, so he didn't need one. So, although the school had given us five guest tickets per person, I'd only claimed three: my mother, Eileen, and Dan. When our family had been taking pictures before my dad and I had left, Eileen had said Dan would meet us there. I wondered what had happened.

Before long, we all sat down, and the ceremony began. There were speeches. Photo slideshows of our class.

Georgia Hale sang Green Day's "Time of Your Life." Even though she'd never been nice, she did have a beautiful voice. It was hard not to feel something as she sang. Maybe it was just because I'd grown up around music my whole life, but I always thought it was one of the most powerful art forms. It was amazing how combinations of notes, instruments, and lyrics could make you feel so much.

Then, our principal spoke. He talked about Y2K, about how we were coming of age at the end of one millennium and the beginning of another. As adults, we were going to define what the 2000s would be. As our class got their diplomas and their families and friends cheered and snapped pictures, I felt like I was in the middle of a movie montage.

I cringed as the principal read my full name, "Marceline

Winifred Lewis." I hated hearing it all together like that but decided it didn't matter. This was probably the last time someone would ever say it.

I walked up to the stage, smiling when I heard Eileen and Maura cheering my name. A strange emotion came over me as I shook the principal's hand and took my diploma. It was bittersweet. High school was over, and now I had the rest of my life ahead of me.

Once everyone had walked the stage and was back in their seats, the principal announced that we were officially graduates of White Lake High School's class of 1999. We turned our tassels and tossed our caps up into the air. We'd done it.

Afterwards, when everyone was milling about outside the school, I caught up with my mom and Eileen. I noticed that my sister's eyes were red, and her makeup was smudged.

"What happened to Dan?" I asked.

In response, Eileen broke down crying. She mumbled off a few things that I didn't catch, except for, "I have to go to the bathroom" before she left.

I looked toward Mom for an answer. "He broke up with her, sweetie."

"Oh ..." I trailed off, more than a little confused. Eileen and Dan had been together for the past six years. Everyone thought they were going to get married. I'd never even guessed that they'd been having problems.

The drive back home was quiet when it should have been filled with laughter. It was dusk, and everything was still. On summer evenings, White Lake took on a surreal quality, almost like we lived on a studio backlot. This only heightened the solemn tenor in the car. I looked at my sister beside me in the backseat, glancing distantly out the window. I couldn't help but feel her grief and wished there was something I could do. I tried reaching out for Eileen's hand, but she pushed me away.

When we got home, she went straight to her room and slammed the door. I felt bad, but I didn't know what to say or do. Things had already been hard for her. Since she'd turned twenty-one and had graduated college, our parents had been on her about moving out. In March, she'd been laid off from her part-time data entry job at a local consulting firm. She'd loved it and had been hoping to continue with them after graduating. It was June, and she still didn't have another job. Now, this.

Mom saw me lingering in the hallway. "Give her some space. You girls are going to have so much fun in New York. Just think of that." I nodded vaguely. She kissed my forehead, told me "congratulations," and wished me good night.

New York. That was hard to think about.

Eileen and I were already having difficulty agreeing on things to do. She'd shot down the Museum of Modern Art and hadn't given me a definitive reason, just that she didn't want to go. We had tickets to *Death of A Salesman*, which she'd only said yes to because I'd agreed to window shop at Saks Fifth Avenue at some point. Other than that, the only thing we'd made solid plans for was Ellis Island and the Statue of Liberty. Past that, I was scared. The Twin Cities were overwhelming enough as it was. It didn't seem right for so many people to be packed together, always in a hurry, for the only nature to be carefully potted trees or a trip to the local park.

That night, my room felt claustrophobic. I eyed the white furniture and the floral curtains. It was in serious need of redecorating. I'd added flourishes, like my posters of *Teen Witch*, *Heathers*, and Nirvana, but as I crawled into bed, I still felt trapped inside skin I was long past ready to shed.

I was lucky to be raised here, in this quiet little slice of Minnesota, but I was restless. White Lake had fewer than ten thousand residents, and though we were about a twenty-minute drive from the Twin Cities without traffic, we might as well have been in our own world.

My parents were hippies back in the seventies and wanted to raise their children with the same values. They'd fallen in love with this house, now surrounded by my mom's carefully tended garden and pond, the first time they'd set foot in it. In my parents' eyes, kids didn't need TVs or computers. To them, anything was better than staring at a screen all day. I only saw movies and the occasional rerun because of Maura. At school, whenever anyone talked about the latest episode of *Dawson's Creek* or *Friends*, I had to nod along and pretend like I knew what they were talking about. It always made me feel isolated.

I took my Discman from my bedside table. Nirvana's *MTV Unplugged,* my favorite CD back then, was still inside. I slipped on the headphones and pressed play, counting on Kurt Cobain to distract me from all I was feeling as I thought about what the future was now going to bring.

The pressure was on for me to find a job as soon as I got back. I'd had a few part-time gigs, mostly babysitting and dog-walking for our neighbors. The summer before, I'd scooped ice cream at a place that had since closed down. I'd wanted to work more, but my parents had always told me that my full-time job was school.

As I listened to Kurt's luscious voice, I felt outside my own body. I thought about how strange it was to be alive in this moment, that one day I was going to fade back into nonexistence. None of us had chosen this life, and yet we were all doomed to the same fate. If I'd had the choice, I would have kept acting, maybe painted more, but that didn't feel like the most realistic career path. There was a way you did things. Get a good, steady job. Provide for your family. That was all most people could ask for. Right?

I was midway through "The Man Who Sold the World," a song that felt like it was cutting right into my soul. I wasn't sure what the fleeting connection on an exhaustive journey it described exactly meant, but maybe that was the point. I felt something, and it was up to me to figure out what that was.

That Sunday, Maura and I celebrated my birthday and her going away. Her parents had given us money to go to a trendy breakfast place in Minneapolis. We planned to make a day of it, shopping and getting our nails done. It would be a little preview of New York.

Maura drove. There was hardly any traffic. These were my favorite kinds of mornings. I looked out at the road, thinking about how, in a few short minutes, the city skyline was going to appear.

"So, how does it feel to be eighteen?" Maura's birthday had been the previous December. She was six months older than me and never let me forget it.

"The same, I guess," I said. It was true. I didn't really feel any different. Only when I thought about how I was an adult in the eyes of the law.

We drove for a little longer. The skyline appeared as it always did, and then we hit some traffic.

"How's Eileen?"

My sister had mostly locked herself in her room the previous two days. "She's still not talking to anyone."

Maura gave a pitied look. "You should both go out to a

fancy restaurant or out dancing or something fun and wild when you're in New York."

I nodded, thinking I would take charge and find something unique that Eileen and I would both enjoy.

After hanging out for most of the day, Maura and I finally had to say goodbye. We hugged. She told me to let her know if I was ever in Tallahassee. She'd for sure be back in White Lake for Thanksgiving. She was going to be busy with classes and moving in, but we would try to make time as often as we could to catch up on the phone.

about the author

Eleanor Wells is a writer, filmmaker, and actress born and raised in Milwaukee, Wisconsin. She graduated from Emerson College in 2017 with a BA in Media Arts Production. She resides in Los Angeles, California and is the author of *All Our Yesterdays* and *Fairytale*.

www.ingramcontent.com/pod-product-compliance
Lightning Source LLC
Chambersburg PA
CBHW050305110726
47899CB00007B/2113